# "I suppose I'll have to marry you."

"I'll have to marry you to save you from the gossipmongers," Brad mused, leaning against the counter, obviously enjoying her discomfort.

"Don't be ridiculous!" Sara used anger to hide the sharp pain his mockingly delivered solution had produced. "I'm sure I can live down one off-color episode."

"First you find me ridiculous, and now I'm an off-color episode," he growled, green fire flashing in his eyes. "There are moments...."

Sara found herself pulled hard against his solid form. Her lips were parted in the beginning of a protest when his mouth found hers, giving the contact an immediate sense of intimacy. Her senses reeled, then sanity was lost in a whirlwind of emotion.

How could she possibly be in love with a man she had known for only a few days?

# The Bonded Heart

## Betsy Page

## Harlequin Books

TORONTO • NEW YORK • LONDON
AMSTERDAM • PARIS • SYDNEY • HAMBURG
STOCKHOLM • ATHENS • TOKYO • MILAN

Original hardcover edition published in 1984
by Mills & Boon Limited

ISBN 0-373-02627-7

Harlequin Romance first edition June 1984

# CHAPTER ONE

WITH difficulty, Sara Manderly guided her car into a parking space nearly two blocks from her desired destination. Her dress, a full skirted, many-petticoated replica of mid-1800s design, flooded the front seat, crowding the steering wheel and making it impossible for her to see her feet.

While her lower body was being so fully covered by what seemed like acres of pale blue satin and lace, her upper half was not nearly so well protected. The neckline of the voluminous creation plunged dangerously low, leaving moon-shaped crescents of her firmly rounded breasts exposed. A tiny pout appeared on her face as she wondered why people put so much material into a skirt and so little into the bodice. Then recalling that it was the exposed ankle or leg which had been taboo in those times long past, she shrugged a lightly-tanned shoulder at human nature and carefully manoeuvred herself out of the car.

The pout hardened into a frown as she stood in the street arranging her skirt and petticoats. How had she allowed Steve to talk her into this charade? Maybe it had been the crack about her sedate lifestyle.

'You're becoming boring, Sis,' he had chided affectionately, his long legs stretched out in front of him as he lounged on the couch in her apartment. 'Whatever happened to your sense of adventure?'

'I focus all of it into my canvases,' she had returned, her observant artist's eye noting the tenseness behind the relaxed façade.

5

'I'll pay you time and a half,' he offered.

Sara hesitated momentarily. She could use the money. Because of budget cuts at the school where she had been an art teacher, she had lost her job at the end of the last term. Unwilling to leave Charleston, she was now living on what she made from selling her paintings and supplementing that from her savings.

'And you've always told me how much you wanted to see the inside of that home,' he continued, sensing an advantage.

'As an invited guest, not as a gatecrasher,' she had stipulated pointedly. 'And I don't understand why you can't use one of your experienced operatives.'

'Brad Garwood knows all my employees and I don't dare go outside of my present operation. This has to be done in the utmost secrecy.'

Taking a sip of coffee, she had smiled playfully. 'If someone had told me that my big, strong, level-headed brother was going to start buying rumours about ghosts and curses in his old age I would have told them they were crazy!'

'At thirty-five, I do not qualify for the senility category and I do not believe in ghosts or curses. Let's just say I'm being cautious.'

His brown eyes, twins of Sara's, had taken on a seriousness which caused her to pause before coming back with another kibitzing response. Steve, eleven years her senior, had always been twice as protective of her as their father, and since Ralph Manderly's death two years earlier had become even more so. For him to ask this kind of a favour was out of character and she found it impossible to flatly refuse.

'Provided I can crash this high society party, what then?'

'All I want you to do is to keep an eye on Brad Garwood.'

'I'm not trained,' she warned.

'You're an artist. Who else could be better trained in the art of observation?' he countered her protest.

'And exactly what am I supposed to be observing?' she sighed resignedly, knowing that she was going to give in sooner or later and it might as well be sooner.

'That I can't tell you.' His eyebrows had come together in a look of perplexity. 'But if you see anything that strikes you as odd or threatening, leave the house immediately. Once you're on the street, pretend you've turned your ankle. Sam will be close by and he'll come running.'

'What with? Garlic and a cross?' she had chided.

'Those are only good for vampires.' Steve's laugh held a hint of embarrassment. 'And remember, you're supposed to remain inconspicuous, so try not to look too pretty.'

Sara had not been able to suppress a smile. Big brothers were great for the morale. It wasn't that she was ugly or plain. But an honest self-appraisal had told her that she was an average-looking young woman who could very easily blend into a crowd. However, there was always the chance that something could go wrong. 'What if I get caught?'

'Lie!' he had commanded.

Lie! The urgency that had been present in his voice when he delivered this order was still with her as she finished arranging her costume. Then, with her stomach churning nervously, she clutched handfuls of satin and petticoats and, attempting to keep the masses of material off the ground, moved swiftly along the dark, deserted side street.

A child's face peered at her from a third-storey window and a tense smile flitted across her countenance. Many of these classically beautiful old structures dated back almost two centuries. Having survived two wars and the great earthquake of 1886, nearly every one of them had its ghost story. Considering the manner in which she was dressed, Sara guessed that she had just reinforced her spectator's belief in the supernatural.

The soft perfume of lilac blooms floated on the quiet night air. But even this gentle scent could not quell her building sense of impending disaster.

Although she would have preferred to seek the shadows along the sidewalks, her fear that her dress would catch and tear on the squat rugged trunks of the palmetto trees lining the avenue kept her in the middle of the street. Originally these chubby palms had been cultivated for defence purposes. Cannonballs were purported to have bounced off their sturdy trunks without causing even the minimum of damage. Now they were grown out of tradition.

Reaching the tip of the Battery, she crossed to the Sea Wall protecting the exclusive homes in this restored section of old Charleston from being flooded. Then with fingers crossed, in the hope that no one would spot her until she was on the wide, flat walking surface, she climbed the short flight of concrete steps to find herself gazing out over the moonlit surface of Charleston Harbour.

Once the waters stretching out before her had been filled with a hundred sailing ships at a time, loading and unloading their cargoes, while their wealthy merchant owners watched from the piazzas of their stately mansions. Now this section of the harbour was mostly a tourist attraction with such historic sites as Fort Sumter, Fort Moultrie, Fort Johnson, Castle Pinckney and Morris Island among others to be visited by vacationers. During the day, visitors wandered along the Sea Wall under the warm South Carolina sun admiring the massive homes that spoke of the opulence and luxury of a time long past.

Not actually past, Sara corrected herself. The Fallons, whose party she was to crash, had money enough to live as well as any of the previous generations of Southern aristocracy.

Ahead of her, horsedrawn vehicles of various shapes and sizes stopped in front of a three-storey red brick residence to discharge passengers attired in period clothing similar to her own. The owners of the local carriage tours must be ecstatic, she mused cynically, a terse half-smile giving her mouth a slightly lopsided appearance. Steve had explained that the invitations had specifically requested the guests to approach the house either in horsedrawn carriages or by foot in keeping with the period costumes. Apparently this was a tradition associated with this particular yearly ball, and those invited cherished their welcome deeply enough to comply.

Sara continued forward slowly. Her plan was to pretend that after alighting from one of the carriages, she had chosen to take a quick stroll along the Sea Wall before joining her companions inside. It was a simple ploy, but she had great faith in simplicity.

From afar she had often admired the three-storey structure which was her final destination. Its triple-tiered piazza and ornate door mouldings decorating the front entrance gave it an air of distinction while a high brickwork wall and wrought iron gates protected the privacy of those who dwelled within. If she had been an invited guest to this gathering of some of Charleston's oldest families, her excitement would have known no bounds. But as it was, she proceeded with a hesitant step.

A breeze blowing in over the water brought a grimace to her face while her hand sought to secure the curls and soft rolls of her carefully styled chestnut hair. Pausing a moment, she arranged her light shawl over her head to prevent any further disarray.

As she came parallel with the house, the palms of her hands began to feel sweaty, and she hoped they would not mark the fabric of her dress. There was a stairway off the wall a few feet ahead of her which she planned to descend and then make her way across the street to the residence. However, as she neared her objective, a carriage which had been obstructing her view of the entrance pulled away, and her heart skipped a beat. Two liveried footmen stood on either side of the iron gate while a very formidable butler guarded the front door checking the invitations of those who entered.

With a sigh Sara admitted defeat. Already aware of the very cloistered attitude of this segment of Charleston society, she had entertained serious doubts about being able to move among them undetected even at so large a gathering. The footmen and butler simply confirmed her reservations. Curiously, however, when she should have felt relieved at not having to go through with the charade, a nagging uneasiness persisted.

Unable to resist, she stood for a moment listening to the music floating out on the night air. Through the second floor windows she caught glimpses of couples dancing to waltzes and tunes popular in an era long dead, and for an instant was transported back in time. Then, noticing a man looking in her direction from a corner window, she turned slowly and moving at the same leisurely pace at which she had approached the house, began to retrace her steps. She hated letting Steve down, but knew it was an outside chance.

Hurried footsteps sounded behind her. Her body tensed as she continued forward, feigning ignorance of another presence.

'You mustn't be so quick to flee,' an unfamiliar male voice admonished, as her pursuer reached her side.

Schooling her features into an expression of polite indulgence, she paused and turned to face the slender blond man, not much older than herself, who had joined her on the Sea Wall. He was dressed in the long waistcoat of the 1800s, and intuitively she guessed that he had been the one watching her from the window.

'I've been observing you for some time,' he smiled, confirming her suspicion. His breath and the slight slur in his speech told her that he was mildly intoxicated, and she hoped he would not create a scene.

'I wasn't fleeing,' she lied. 'I simply wanted some fresh air.'

Disregarding her response, he continued in an amused vein, 'I'm certain I've been introduced to every eligible female near my age, give or take six years, and yet I know we've never met.'

'I'm a distant cousin?' she suggested dubiously, realising that he meant her no harm and was merely finding her an interesting diversion.

'I've met all of them too,' he laughed.

'Then, obviously, I'm a ghost from the past and it's time for me to vanish.' Turning as she spoke, Sara moved purposefully away, assuming that the man would return to the party with an amusing antedote with which to entertain the other guests.

This, however, was not the case. 'I've never conversed with a ghost before,' he mused, falling into step beside her. 'Let me introduce myself. I'm Marc Fallon.'

A sudden wariness came over her as she again paused to face the man fully. 'You're the one throwing the party.'

'No.' He held up a hand in protest. 'My sister, Monica, is throwing the party. I am simply a tolerant bystander.'

'More intolerant than tolerant, I would say,' Sara commented, catching the hint of disfavour in his tone. 'Don't you like dressing up?'

'I don't mind the dressing up part and I do have a very tolerant nature. However, my sister has pushed me to the limit. For the past two months she's made everyone's life a misery while she's made her preparations for this ball and I'm dying to throw a wench into the proceedings.'

'You mean a wrench,' Sara corrected.

'No—a wench,' he smiled mischievously.

'That's rather a dangerous move, don't you think?' she questioned, catching on to what he was hinting at and uncertain as to how to proceed.

'I prefer to think of it as adventurous, rather in keeping with the spirit of our costumes. Consider it an attempt at reminiscence: an effort to recapture the lost romance of the times. You can be the mysterious Southern belle who appears at the ball and afterwards everyone discovers that no one knew who you were.'

'But you don't know anything about me,' she cautioned. The man seemed sincere, still she was not certain she should trust him.

'You aren't a jewel thief?' he demanded, raising his hand to his heart in mock horror.

'No,' she smiled indulgently.

'Then I assume you're a reporter from one of those yellow tabloids they sell in the grocery stores and that you're carrying a hidden camera in a cigarette lighter.'

Common sense told Sara to deny the accusation and continue on her way. But she had made Steve a promise, and Marc Fallon appeared to be willing to unknowingly help her achieve her goal. 'Aren't you worried about becoming a social outcast once your association with me is discovered?' she questioned.

'I'm a Fallon,' he reminded her, the amused gleam again sparking in his eyes. 'I may be referred to as a black sheep or incorrigible, but never an outcast. Besides, I'm also a cad. Once I have you inside, I plan to desert you to the wolves and see how you fare.'

Any reservations, Sara might have had about causing the man any trouble vanished. 'In that case, I accept.'

A triumphant smile lit his face. 'Then I insist we enter in style.' Taking her arm, he turned her around and began walking her in the direction from which they had just come. Continuing past his home, they descended the Sea Wall and crossed over to Battery Park. Leading her around the edge of this small quiet island of greenery, he did not stop until they were out of sight of the house. 'You wait here,' he directed, positioning her near one of the cannons decorating the landscape. 'And don't talk to strangers!'

Sara could hear him laughing to himself as he marched out into the street and hailed one of the empty carriages. Again it occurred to her that it would be prudent to escape now before she was in so deep she could not get out. But an indefinably vague inner sense held her there. 'I must be more affected by Steve's power of suggestion than I thought,' she muttered.

Money changed hands between Marc and the driver. Then, re-claiming her, he led her to the open-air conveyance. Once she was seated, he chose the seat next to her and motioned the driver to urge his horse into action. 'I seem to have been doing most of the talking,' he said, as they began their slow progress around the block. 'As a consequence, I don't believe you've mentioned your name.'

'It's Sara,' she smiled.

'Sara . . . ?' he prompted.

She hesitated, recalling Steve's terse instructions.

Placing a silencing finger on her lips, Marc shook his head. 'Rather than have a lie between us, I shall call you Cindy—that's short for Cinderella. It's only fitting and proper. And I shall be your Fairy Godfather. I've provided you with a horse and carriage and am seeing that you get to the ball. You may remain as late as you like, but I'll warn you to stay away from my sister. There! Now I don't have to think of myself as a cad. Cinderella's Fairy Godmother didn't stay to protect her. Therefore it's only fitting that I don't protect you.'

'Perhaps I'll find a Prince Charming to protect me,' she bantered, nervousness again causing her palms to sweat.

'And perhaps I've miscast myself,' he mused, giving her an appraising glance. Then with a resigned sigh he added, 'If only I wasn't so fearful of Monica's wrath.'

His continued reference to his sister's temper was making Sara decidedly edgy. Again she was tempted to escape, but before she could tell the coachman to stop and let her out it was too late, they had come to a gentle halt outside the wrought iron gates.

As Marc descended from the carriage and paused to help her alight, the footmen's faces took on a startled expression, but neither spoke. The butler, who obviously had more experience with his young employer's eccentricities, allowed his expression to waver only momentarily before he said, 'Good evening, Mr Marc.'

'Nice to see you again so soon, Blackwell,' Marc frowned, his demeanour that of a slightly drunk Lord of the Manor. 'This is Cindy, a wandering ghost, whom you will not mention to my sister for fear of being haunted the rest of your days.'

'Yes, sir.' The man's manner, while remaining stiffly polite, held a touch of indulgent disapproval, and Sara flushed. She guessed she would be one of the major topics of discussion in the servants' quarters after the ball and all that was said would not necessarily be kind.

And Blackwell was only the beginning. The moment they were through the door and into the entrance hall, they were accosted by an elderly woman in a grey lace creation designed to accent an emerald and diamond necklace glittering around her neck. Recalling Marc's query as to whether she was a jewel thief, Sara realised that the man was willing to risk a great deal to satisfy his own whims.

'My goodness, Marc, who is this lovely young lady?' the woman questioned, her eyes travelling over Sara searchingly as she attempted to fit the newcomer into one of the families of this tight little society.

'This is Cindy, Mrs Leison.' To Sara's relief, Marc maintained a straight face and a polite air. 'She's a distant cousin.'

'Distant cousin?' the woman coaxed, determined to gather more information.

'Yes, all the way from Montana,' he quipped, then added, 'If you'll excuse me, I must find the bar. I haven't had a drink for nearly an hour.'

'That young man imbibes far too much,' Mrs Leison remarked, watching his departing back.

'Yes,' Sara agreed, then before the woman could resume her probing added, 'If you'll excuse me too, I want to powder my nose.' Forsaking the downstairs sitting room and dining room where a large buffet had been laid out, she moved towards the stairs, hoping that the woman would not follow. For a moment Mrs Leison looked indecisive, then as a new group of guests arrived, returned to her position near the door to continue her private inventory of arrivals.

On the second floor, the room fronting on the harbour ran the entire width of the house and with the furniture removed, provided an excellent area for dancing. A pianist and two violinists provided the music as the women, in their flowing gowns, swayed gracefully in the discreet embraces of their white gloved partners. Watching them, Sara sensed an air of romance so lacking in the clubs of today where couples wrapped themselves so tightly in each other's arms that it gave the impression of necking rather than dancing.

She had never met Brad Garwood, but Steve had shown her a photograph of the man. His face, while not actually handsome, had been decidedly interesting, and she wondered if his eyes were really as green as they had appeared in the picture.

They were! She caught a flash of emerald as he moved across the dance floor with a slender black-haired beauty in his arms. Edging into one of the darker corners of the softly lit room, she watched the couple. The woman was smiling up at him, flirting playfully, while his expression indicated that he was enjoying the attention.

'Monica appears to be willing to go to any lengths to retain Cyprus Point,' a middle-aged woman dressed in a pale pink gown remarked pointedly to her female companion. They were standing only a foot or so away from where Sara was attempting to blend into the drapery, making it impossible for her not to eavesdrop.

'I wouldn't call marrying Brad Garwood "going to any lengths",' the companion returned with an indulgent smile. 'If I were twenty years younger, it's a sacrifice I would be willing to make.'

'But he's a Yankee,' the woman in pink protested behind her fan, the word 'Yankee' coming out with an air of profanity.

'And the war ended over a hundred years ago,' her companion countered.

'There are some things that time simply cannot erase,' came the haughty reply. 'Hanna Fallon would turn over in her grave if she knew her granddaughter was allowing herself to be courted by a Yankee.'

'I will admit it's a good thing she's not alive to witness them together, nor to see the day when a Yankee will own Cyprus Point,' the second woman conceded.

'Provided he survives to sign the papers.' There was an ominous tone in the woman's voice which caused Sara to shiver and redirect her full attention to the brown-haired man who was now leading his partner to the doorway.

The music had stopped and the musicians were laying aside their instruments to indicate that they intended to take a break. Before any attention could be directed towards her by the onlookers who had been watching the dancers or by any dancers joining friends along the perimeter of the dance floor, Sara slipped out of her corner and made her way towards the door. Following Brad Garwood and Monica Fallon at a discreet distance, she crossed the wide hallway and entered a second large room arranged as a sitting room for those who needed a respite from the dancing but did not want to go downstairs.

The couple had joined a small group of people and it looked as if Monica was introducing Brad Garwood to the others, giving the impression that he was not well known among the guests. Except by reputation, Sara amended mentally, knowing that, like the ladies she had overheard, the members of this close society not only knew everyone else's business but considered it their duty to do so and to have opinions regarding the propriety of one another's behaviour.

Coming to a halt a few feet away, she found herself

intrigued by the man's profile. There was a shrewdness about the features which gave the impression that he was used to being in command of any given situation and would be a dangerous man to cross. Perhaps it was the sharpness of definition in the bone structure, she mused, forgetting to be cautious and staring at him forthrightly. Unexpectedly a pair of sea-green eyes fell on her, forcing her to turn quickly away and bringing a selfconscious flush to her cheeks. She wasn't supposed to attract his attention.

Smiling at an elderly gentleman as if he were an old acquaintance, she accepted a drink from the tray of a passing waiter and edged her way towards the fireplace. Catching bits and pieces of conversation, it suddenly dawned on her just how well these people knew one another. Sensing danger if she remained in this cloistered environment, she changed direction and moved back towards the door.

'Careful, Cindy,' Marc whispered, appearing suddenly as if from nowhere and startling her. 'If I were you, I wouldn't stay too long in the same room with my sister.'

Schooling her face into a smile as if he had just made a clever quip, Sara responded in a hushed hiss, 'I was just on my way out.'

Saluting her with his drink, he passed on by to be greeted by a mother and daughter who were obviously interested in making him a part of their family group.

Brad, meanwhile, had ordered Bourbon on the rocks which was being delivered to him by one of the servants, while Monica was being summoned by a group of women on the far side of the room. Leaving his side, she went to speak to her friends. Brad remained where he was talking earnestly to a man near his own age.

As Sara glanced towards him a final time it was to

discover him watching her over his companion's shoulder. A nervous twinge threatened the carefully controlled indifference of her expression and she quickly completed her exit.

The piazza was her next destination. Each of the two rooms in use had several windows opening on to this long, roofed porch and she decided that the safest place for her was outside in the dark looking in. The other couples who had wandered out to enjoy the soft Southern night were so enthralled with one another that they paid her no heed and she was able to blend in with the shadows undisturbed.

When she was again able to observe Brad Garwood, Monica had rejoined him and was leading him back to the dance floor. Curiously, as if he instinctively knew he was being watched, he glanced towards Sara's newest observation post forcing her to duck back quickly.

Crossing over to one of the windows opening onto the ballroom, she saw him dancing first with Monica and then with several other ladies as the dark-haired socialite played the proper hostess and danced with her other male guests. There was a virility about the man that struck her almost like a physical force. His skin was tanned a healthy copper. From Steve she knew that although he was a talented architect, he spent as much time on his construction sites as he did at his drawing board. He was a big man, as tall as Steve and very near Steve's age, she guessed. His broad shoulders were evidence that he did not merely watch his labourers work but joined them in their efforts.

While it was difficult to envisage him being in danger, it was not the least bit difficult envisaging him as being dangerous. 'You're romanticising,' she cautioned herself in a hushed murmur as she shifted her weight from one foot to the other and cursed the uncomfortable shoes she had been forced to wear in keeping with her period costume.

And it wasn't only her feet. Her legs were beginning to cramp from the almost immobile stance she had maintained for the past hour—not to mention the nuisance caused by the occasional mosquito. Luckily the harbour breezes kept that population down to a minimum, or the next day she would have looked as if she had the measles. With her shawl wrapped securely around her arms and shoulders for protection, she leaned back on to the porch railing to give her legs a rest. Although the structure creaked ever so lightly, it seemed firm enough, and she was grateful for the relief. There was a bench nearby, but the light from the windows fell on it and she did not want to risk moving from her shadowed position.

Detective work, she decided, attempting to wiggle her toes in the confining shoes, was not only boring but decidedly uncomfortable. Well, not exactly boring, she amended, finding it difficult to associate that word with Brad Garwood.

Feeling smugly safe from observation, she was not worried when she lost track of her prey until a sudden warning sense caused her to glance towards the french doors leading on to the piazza. The man had passed through them and was moving purposefully towards her. The railing creaked again as she shifted position slightly, feigning an intense interest in the darkened harbour.

'The view is much better from inside,' his deep, gravelly tones sliced the air between them.

Breathing deeply to steady her nerves, Sara turned slowly to face him and smiling politely, said, 'I don't think so. Even with only the moonlight I can see Fort Sumter from here.'

'I'm not a man who enjoys playing games,' he scowled.

Holding his voice low added an intimidating edge to his speech, and Sara's back stiffened defiantly. 'I don't understand what you're talking about,' she returned, rising from the railing and smoothing out the material of her skirt as if she found this entire conversation boring and intended to leave.

His eyes narrowed. She had been sequestered in a corner and instead of moving aside to let her pass, he took a step forward, causing his legs to meet the hem of her voluminous skirt. Then to secure his advantage he placed a hand on the pillar to her left. With no room to pass him on the side by the window, she was trapped. 'You've been watching me all evening, and I find it a decidedly uncomfortable sensation,' he said coolly.

Steve had told her to lie, but she guessed a denial would do no good. Her instincts told her that Brad Garwood was not the kind of man who could be played for a fool. Unconsciously, she licked her lips nervously, then forcing a smile, said in her best coquettish manner, 'I apologise if I've caused you any discomfort. I do confess to having been observing you. I'm an artist and I find your face a very interesting study.'

Although his voice took on a gentler tone, a strong note of scepticism told her that he had not totally bought the half-truth. 'I don't believe we've been introduced. I'm Brad Garwood.'

'I'm pleased to meet you, Mr Garwood,' she smiled, hoping that in the dark he would not read the panic in her eyes.

For a long moment, he stood patiently waiting, but as the silence continued he frowned darkly. 'It's your turn.'

'I'm Cindy, a distant cousin of the Fallons,' she stammered, her entire body rebelling against lying to this man, causing her to feel confused and frustrated.

'Cindy,' he repeated the name as if testing its authenticity. 'Somehow you don't strike me as a "Cindy". However, it would be ungallant of me to call so lovely a lady a liar. Instead, I'll ask you to dance.'

'I'm not really in the mood,' she managed, her words coming with surprising calm.

'I insist.' There was no compromise in his tone. Reaching out, he captured her hand.

The contact seemed almost to burn. Startled by her reaction to the man's touch and fearful of exposure, Sara attempted to pull away. As she took a step backward, her full weight pressed against the wooden railing. Suddenly a sharp splintering sound filled the air as a portion of the structure gave way. Losing her balance, she would have fallen to the ground below except for the firm hold Brad Garwood had on her hand. As a shriek of terror escaped her lips, she felt herself being jerked hard against the stone wall of his chest. Standing in the secure circle of his embrace, her arms wrapped tightly around his solid form, she had the sensation of being completely safe and protected. Then as the voices of others gathering around them reached her brain, she flushed with embarrassment and, pushing away from him, managed to choke out a thank-you.

'Are you all right?' he questioned, his voice showing true concern.

'Yes,' she murmured, meeting the velvet green of his eyes and suddenly feeling shaky all over again, but this time for a much different reason.

'Grandma must have had a great deal more gypsy blood in her than we ever knew,' Marc Fallon noted cryptically, materialising beside her. 'She always hated outsiders.'

Before Sara or Brad could react to this statement, Monica came through the doorway demanding to know what had happened.

'Cindy had a bit of a scare,' Marc explained nonchalantly as the small crowd parted to allow their hostess access to the heart of the scene. 'And now I intend to take her inside and find her a brandy. I'm a great believer in alcohol for medicinal purposes, among others.'

'Cindy?' Monica's voice was a sharp question hanging on the air as Marc took Sara's hand and literally dragged her after him into the house and then down the stairs.

'I think perhaps it's time for Cinderella to flee the ball,' he suggested with a conspiratorial smile.

'I think so too,' she agreed. 'And thanks for the little added help FG.' With a quick wink, she hurried out the front door and down the sidewalk.

A man walking a dog on the Sea Wall quickened his pace, crossing the street ahead of where she was and then slowing to an easy gait. 'I saw what happened,' he said in hushed tones as she came abreast. 'You all right?'

'I'm fine, Sam,' she assured him in the same muted tones.

'These homes have been around for a long time. You'd have thought they would have checked those railings before throwing a big party like this one,' he commented with a disapproving shake of his head as he slowed his pace once again to allow her to move ahead of him before he changed direction and started back the way he had come.

The dog barked and Sara heard Sam's hushed tones quieting him, but did not turn around to see what had caught the dog's interest. She still felt shaky and her whole attention was focused on getting home, the quicker the better.

Twenty minutes later, as she climbed the rickety out-side staircase to her second-floor apartment, the remem-bered sensation of falling as the railing gave way behind her caused an uncontrolled shiver. This was followed by a deep fiery glow as the memory of being held firmly against Brad Garwood's long form filled her senses.

Dismissing this disturbingly acute reaction to the man as the result of shock and heightened emotion brought on by her near fatal accident, she let herself into her apart-ment and put on some hot water for a cup of tea. It had been a long evening.

Sitting down on the couch, she unfastened the shoes which had been the bane of her existence during the entire evening and slipping them off, luxuriated in the feel of freedom from the pain of pinched toes. Then, standing up, she began to work on unbuttoning the dress. A loud knocking interrupted the process. Fastening the chain securely, she opened the door a crack to find Brad Gar-wood standing on the small landing, a scowl on his face. 'Open the door,' he demanded.

'No!' her refusal came out sharply as she held the door with one hand and the dress in place with the other.

'I'm not leaving until I get some answers. I'll stand here and pound on your door all night, if that's what it takes.' The anger darkening his features told her that he meant to carry out this threat.

A resigned sigh escaped from Sara. She couldn't afford to let him make a racket. Her apartment was the second floor of a private residence with her landlady occupying the bottom floor. Although she still had six months re-maining on her lease, the sudden impending return of Mrs Wynn's son and his wife had given the woman a strong desire to evict Sara and regain the full use of her home. Over the past few weeks, she had professed to having developed an allergy to Sara's oil paints and complained that the fumes were keeping her awake at night. She accused Sara of throwing wild parties whenever a friend came over for coffee and swore she was going to have the phone disconnected if it rang after nine in the evening. Sara knew she was fighting a losing battle but was determined to hold on until the last moment. This was not only the cheapest place she could find in a decent neighbourhood, but it had come fully furnished; not that the furnishings were anything to brag about, but they were free and liveable with. 'I have to close the door a minute to unfasten the chain,' she said, following her words with actions.

'I warn you, I'm dangerous when provoked,' he growled, slamming the door closed behind him as she backed away. Coming to an abrupt halt, he studied her contemptuously. 'You look like Scarlett O'Hara fearing that she's going to be ravished by the enemy. Either go and change or refasten that dress, but stop standing there halfway in and halfway out.'

Brown fury flashed in Sara's eyes. 'I didn't invite you to come barging into my home so you'll have to excuse me for not being dressed for company.'

'I'll excuse you for nothing until I get some answers,' he returned drily, his eyes never leaving her as she struggled to hold the dress in place and maintain her dignity.

The whistle on the teapot sounded, forcing her to go into the kitchen and switch off the stove. He was blocking the doorway when she turned to go out. 'I thought you said you wanted me to change,' she glared, anger masking the panic building inside. He was a big man.

'Maybe I've changed my mind.' His eyes travelled down to the cleavage between her breasts, bringing a dark flush to her skin.

'Mr Garwood, either you get out of my way or I start screaming,' she threatened. 'My landlady is a light sleeper and calls the police at the least little sound of a disturbance.'

Slowly a cynical smile curled his lips. 'I don't know about you,' he said, giving her room to pass, 'but I do have a reputation to protect.'

Her chin shot up. How dared he insult her! 'You can wait in there.' She indicated the living room with a shrug of her shoulder as she walked with her back straight and her head held high down to her bedroom.

Once there, she changed out of the dress and into a pair of jeans and a tee-shirt. Dressed in her normal attire, she began to feel more in control. Determined to insist that the man leave, she marched down to the living room, only to find that he was not there. He was not in the kitchen either. Her first reaction was one of relief, assuming that he had become bored with his cat-and-mouse game and gone home. Then her intuition took over and she knew that assumption was only wishful thinking. Retracing her steps down the hall, she went into the room she used for a studio and found him standing in front of her easel with the cloth raised examining the almost finished seascape beneath.

'It would appear that being an artist is the only thing you didn't lie to me about . . . Sara Manderly.' He turned to face her, his expression black. 'Unless you lied even about that and the woman who signed the finished works in this room is your room-mate.'

Without her billowing dress and high-heeled shoes, her slight five-foot-five-inch frame seemed even smaller beside his large bulk, but her brother was a big man too and she refused to allow size to intimidate her. 'I live alone,' she snapped back, his sarcasm momentarily clouding her common sense. As soon as the words were out she wished she had professed to having a room-mate asleep in the bedroom. Angry with herself for letting the man unnerve her, she decided to take the offensive. 'How did you find me?'

'When you left the house in such a rush I was close behind,' he replied, releasing the covering and allowing it to fall back into place. 'At first I only wanted to be certain you were capable of getting home safely. You'd been pretty shaken up. Then I spotted you talking to Sam and decided to follow you and get to the truth.'

'You couldn't have followed me on foot and I would have noticed a horse and carriage,' she muttered suspiciously.

'Being an uncouth Yankee, I'd driven my car and parked it down the block, then walked to the party. I was behind the wheel before you ever turned into your side street to collect your vehicle.'

'I see.' She met his angry stare with equal hostility.

'And now about you, Miss Manderly. I have a Chief of Security by that name. Is it possible that the two of you are related?'

'Steve's my brother.' She saw no sense in lying at this point.

'And unless Sam's moved recently, he travelled quite a distance out of his way to walk his dog.'

Neither confirming nor denying this statement, she turned away from the man and went back to the kitchen where she continued to make her tea. Assuming he had all the answers he needed to figure out the rest, she was surprised when he did not leave the apartment but came to stand in the doorway and watch her. 'Won't Monica be missing you?' she frowned.

'Monica has a house full of guests. If she asks, I'll

simply explain that you were a bit shaken up and I saw you home.'

'And what if she asks you where home was?'

'You're good at games,' he mused cynically. 'I suppose it would be more prudent to tell her that I saw you to your car and then went for a walk on the Sea Wall and stopped for a smoke.'

'It's turning into a very long walk and a whole pack of cigarettes,' she commented pointedly.

'Aren't you going to offer me a cup of tea?' he questioned drily, refusing to take the hint.

'No.' Her response was firm. 'I want you to leave.' She was finding the man's presence increasingly disturbing and wanted very much to be rid of him.

'Not yet.' It was as if he was waiting for something to happen.

Sara stood watching him in a frosty silence, uncertain how to proceed, when a second loud knocking startled her, causing her to spill her tea.

Brad, on the other hand, did not seem the least bit surprised and while she mopped up the counter with a towel, he answered the door. 'I've been here half an hour,' she heard him growl, 'I expected you much sooner.'

'I was in bed when Sam called,' Steve's familiar tones drifted into the kitchen.

'You had Sam call Steve?' she questioned, staring at Brad incredulously as she joined the men in the hall.

'No. I simply assumed Sam would call him after he followed me here,' he replied matter-of-factly, keeping his attentioned focused on Steve. 'And now I want a complete explanation of this evening's fiasco.'

'I could use a cup of coffee,' Steve smiled encouragingly towards Sara as he led Brad into the living room.

'Then you can make it yourself,' she snapped back,

refusing to be eased out of the way while the men talked.

Throwing her an exasperated glance, Steve motioned for Brad to be seated. When the man refused, he too remained standing. 'Ever since you decided to purchase the Cyprus Point Plantation I haven't been able to rest easy,' he explained in a calm tone. 'I felt you needed someone to keep an eye on you, and since I knew you wouldn't tolerate the idea, I decided to do it covertly.'

'So you sent your sister?' Brad's voice was liquid ice.

'You know all of my other operatives and I didn't want to go outside my present organisation,' Steve continued in the same unruffled manner, obviously used to Brad's intimidating manner.

'And what if she'd got caught sneaking in? Monica's not above calling the police and having her arrested,' Brad demanded. 'In fact it's common knowledge that she always insists on having trespassers prosecuted. That's why she has so little trouble with uninvited guests.'

'I admit it was a calculated risk, but I was relying on Sara's good judgment.'

Over Steve's shoulder, Brad threw Sara a look that said he questioned if she had any judgment at all, and her chin shot up defiantly.

'Besides, she didn't sneak in,' Steve continued, ignoring the wordless interaction. 'According to Sam, she was escorted in by Marc Fallon.'

Again Brad's attention turned to Sara. 'Does he know why you were there?'

'No.' She met his gaze squarely. 'He thought I was a reporter for one of these scandal sheets. Apparently his sister had got on his nerves lately and he decided it would be a great joke to foist me upon her.'

'I guess I should be grateful for that,' he growled, then returned his attention to Steve. 'Do you realise the damage you could have caused if anyone had got wind that my Chief of Security was worried about my personal safety? If the suspicion arose that I might not be around to fulfil my commitments, my business could be in serious trouble.'

'I realise that,' Steve continued to face the man levelly. 'That's why I didn't go outside our present organisation.'

'I wasn't aware that your sister was on our payroll.' Brad's eyes travelled over her body as if memorising every detail for future reference. Sara shifted uncomfortably but stood her ground.

'She isn't. Like I said before, you would have recognised one of my regulars, just as you recognised Sam.'

'So you sent a novice, and she not only nearly got herself caught but was almost killed,' he scowled.

A look of remorse spread over Steve's features as he directed his attention towards Sara. 'I heard about the railing. I'm sorry, Sis.'

'It's all right,' she assured him. 'But don't ask for any more favours!'

A flash of camaraderie passed between the brother and sister, and Steve threw her a wink.

Brad had watched the interplay, his expression remaining cool. 'I suppose no harm has been done. But I don't want a replay of this. If I'd known you could be taken in by ghost stories and rumours I would have thought twice about hiring you, Manderly.'

'It's not the ghost stories. It's the facts,' Steve defended himself, his manner businesslike and firm. 'Two people have tried to buy Cyprus Point and both of them are dead.'

'One was an old woman with a serious heart condition who should have died years earlier and the other was an alcoholic who ran his car off of a cliff while driving under the influence. It was merely a coincidence that both were trying to purchase Cyprus Point.'

'Possibly . . . probably,' Steve admitted. 'But I had a gut instinct about the ball tonight. Not only have you lived in Charleston for less than six years but you're a Yankee. For most of us common Southerners, being from north of the Mason-Dixon line is not considered a sin, but when mixing with those who consider themselves a part of the old Southern aristocracy, the origin of your birth is a different matter. That bunch is so closed, a whole family has to die out before they let a new one in, and then it has to be a family whose members have been Southerners for a century or better. For you to have been invited to one of their gatherings was totally out of character.'

'For Pete's sake, is that what you were basing your suspicions on?' Sara demanded, her hands coming up to rest on her hips as she shook her head in disgust. 'He was invited because Monica Fallon has set her sights on having him for a husband.' Monica's name came out sounding slightly sour, bringing a flush to Sara's cheeks, since she had meant merely to state a fact and not offer a hint of an opinion.

'No kidding?' Steve glanced questioningly at Brad, a half smile on his face, while Brad raised a noncommittal eyebrow.

In that moment Sara realised that, in spite of their heated exchange, the two men liked and respected one another.

Suddenly the sound of knocking again filled the air. This time it came from the door which opened on to the staircase leading to the downstairs portion of the house, and Sara groaned. A visit from Mrs Wynn was the last thing she needed tonight. The knocking sounded again, more insistent this time, and she opened the door to find her landlady standing there with a look of triumph on her face.

'I refuse to put up with any more cars careening in and out of my driveway or coming to screeching halts in front of my house or the men clopping around up here at all hours of the day and night! Tonight has been the final straw! Either you agree to be out of here by the end of the week or I'll call the police and have you arrested for disturbing the peace!'

Knowing that the woman would carry through with her threat, Sara sighed resignedly. 'All right, I'll move.'

'By the end of the week,' Mrs Wynn repeated her stipulation firmly.

'By the end of the week,' Sara confirmed coolly.

Nodding her approval, the woman then left, slamming the door behind her.

'I'm sorry, Sis,' Steve apologised. 'I forgot you were having trouble.'

Normally an even-tempered girl, Sara had reached her breaking point. 'Just get out, both of you,' she commanded.

Brad Garwood moved towards the door, the look on his face saying he was glad to be leaving this Bohemian dive.

Steve, however, hung back. 'I'm sorry, Sis. You know you can come stay with Helen and me.'

'Out!' she snapped more sharply, and with a grimace he obeyed.

Mrs Wynn had made it sound as if Sara had men callers every night, and as she locked the door it bothered her that Brad Garwood had got the impression that she was wanton in her behaviour. With a mental shrug she tried telling herself that it didn't matter what the man thought, but for some reason it did. In fact she had a tremendous urge to cry. Deciding that she was simply tired and still a little shaken up from her near-accident, she went to bed. Surely in the morning life would look brighter.

# CHAPTER TWO

RISING early to catch the morning light, Sara again dressed in jeans and a tee-shirt. Carrying her cup of coffee into her studio, she pulled on one of Steve's cast-off shirts which she used as a smock and attempted to finish the canvas now on her easel. It only needed a few touch-up strokes and then she would be free to spend all her time searching for a new place to live.

Being a realist, she had been looking off and on ever since Mrs Wynn had mentioned that her son and his wife were returning to Charleston. Her search, however, had proved futile, and she didn't suspect that the housing situation was going to change in the next day or two. Probably she would be forced to move in with Steve and Helen temporarily and this she hated to do. She and Helen got along very well, but with two young children to handle, her sister-in-law did not need an indefinite house guest.

The thought of going back to Florida to live with her mother flashed distastefully through her mind. It wasn't that she didn't love Ida, she simply couldn't put up with the woman's interference, which had increased to dramatic proportions since her father's death. For the first year following Ralph Manderly's death, when Ida wasn't calling or writing to offer advice to both her daughter and her daughter-in-law, she was visiting them until both Sara and Helen found it nearly impossible to remain civil. In an effort to maintain family harmony, they had finally convinced Ida that she needed to broaden her horizons and that travel was the answer. At the present time Ida was in the Mediterranean on a cruise.

But it wasn't only Ida. Sara had fallen in love with Charleston. Its softness, its history, its charm all blended together to produce a special flavour found nowhere else.

Then there was her art. She had finally begun to gain a reputation locally. Just recently she had convinced one of the more prominent galleries to display her work on a regular basis.

And then there was her niece and nephew. She would miss them terribly if she left. Her mouth formed a determined line. There were too many reasons to stay. She just couldn't leave.

Curiously, with that thought still strong in her mind, Brad Garwood's face crossed her consciousness. 'It's his features,' she muttered. 'They're artistically appealing to me.' Frowning at herself, she attempted to vanquish the disturbing image. But as she began to work the final greens into her painting, his eyes returned to haunt her. A warm glow filled her as she remembered their velvet softness following her near fall. The glow, however, turned to ice as that memory faded and was replaced by his final contemptuous glance as he had left her apartment. Angrily she forced herself to concentrate on her work.

Finishing the painting, she left it uncovered to dry and curling up on the couch started through the rental listings in the newspaper. Several phone calls later she was feeling totally depressed when a knock sounded on her door. Assuming it was Steve coming to apologise again, she didn't bother with the chain.

'Good morning, Miss Manderly,' Brad Garwood's impersonal tones greeted her surprised countenance.

In the daylight, she wasn't certain if it was the startling green of his eyes or the sharp definition of his features that was the most fascinating. But only in an artistic sense, she qualified mentally.

'You're staring at me again,' he reprimanded as if speaking to a child.

'I'm sorry,' she stammered, then chided herself for letting the man unnerve her once again.

'Are you going to ask me in, or do we conduct our business on your doorstep?' he continued in an indulgent vein.

'I didn't know we had any business,' she said coolly, regaining her equilibrium.

Ignoring her less-than-hospitable manner, he completed his entrance, closing the door behind him. 'I want to apologise for the trouble I caused you last night. I'm sure finding another place to live can be a nuisance.'

'You could call it that,' she replied, trailing after him into the living room, infuriated with the way he made himself at home. Then remembering her manners even if he had forgotten his, she added, 'However, your apology is accepted. After all, I suppose I do owe you my life. I could have been seriously injured falling on to that brick courtyard.'

'I'm glad you realise that.' He was regarding her with a darkly shuttered gaze she found disquieting, and her back stiffened defensively. 'I gather you don't work for your brother on a regular basis.'

'I don't work for my brother at all,' she corrected sharply. 'Last night was the first and last time I'll help him. I would have refused to do even that, but he's normally so overly protective of me I felt certain he had to be seriously concerned to ask for such a favour. I had no way of knowing that his concern was unfounded.'

He stared at her coolly for a long moment as if weighing her words, then said, 'Although I find your artistic skill to my liking, I've always been under the impression that it's difficult for an artist to support himself or herself on their art alone.'

'Excluding wealthy sponsors or a developed reputation, you're correct.' As she caught the suggestive edge in his voice, a hostile flush began to redden her cheeks.

'Could it be that one of the reasons you succumbed to your brother's request that you attend the ball last night was that you thought you might meet someone who would be willing to sponsor you?'

'No!' she glared up at him, brown fury meeting green ice. 'I prefer to take care of myself.'

'And what exactly do you do to take care of yourself?' he persisted, his attitude one of a person who has come for a purpose.

'What exactly do you think I do?' Sara challenged, her pride keeping her chin high and her back straight.

'I was wondering if you cooked.'

'Cooked?' She stared at him incredulously.

'I'm in need of a housekeeper,' he elaborated. 'The person wouldn't have to do any heavy cleaning—I have a service that comes in once a week for that. But I need someone to see that the rooms are kept straightened, the laundry is done on time, and to prepare meals.'

'I would think you could find any number of suitable people for the position,' Sara remarked suspiciously.

'It's a live-in position,' he continued, disregarding her comment. 'There's a bedroom with a private bath off the kitchen, and the person has to be willing to adjust to an irregular schedule.'

Sara had the distinct impression that they were discussing something quite different from cooking and cleaning. 'Like I said, I would think there would be any number of people willing, to take the job.'

'I'm willing to pay you six hundred dollars a month plus bed and board. You'll have Thursday evenings and every other weekend off. There's a room on the third floor with a skylight which you could use as a studio.'

Irritated by his confident manner, she became even more rigid. 'No, thank you,' she refused firmly, adding sarcastically, 'Don't you think offering a person like myself a position in your home is a pretty steep price to pay simply as an apology? What will your friends think?'

'I rarely let what other people think influence me,' he replied coolly, his eyes darkening to a curious jade green. 'However, since you refuse to cook and clean for me, perhaps we can work out a different kind of arrangement.'

Erasing the distance between them with one long stride, his fingers closed like tempered steel around her wrists as her hands came up to ward off his advance. Retaining his hold, he forced her arms behind her, trapping her securely while moulding her to his long form.

As she started to protest, his mouth covered hers possessively, her parted lips giving the kiss an instant sensation of intimacy.

Panicked, she twisted against his taut frame. He held her easily, and as the muscular impression of his thighs burned into her, a sensual excitement so strong it caused her to shiver ignited a level of emotion she had never before experienced.

Involuntarily, as if her body had a will of its own, her struggle, which was supposed to be relaying a message of repulsion, seemed instead to be caressing him in the most intimate manner. Terrified by her reactions, she froze into immobility.

A low moan escaped his lips as he deserted her mouth to taste her neck. 'I was enjoying your active resistance,' he murmured, nipping her earlobe.

'Let go of me!' she hissed, fighting the awful weakening effect he was having on her.

Ignoring her demand, he kissed the pulse throbbing in her neck. 'I don't think that's really what you want.'

'Yes, it is,' she choked out, feeling as if she was on the edge of an abyss and in grave peril of falling in. Desperate to regain her freedom, she kicked his shin as hard as she could with her bare foot. 'Ouch!' she cried, having caused him very little pain while inflicting a great deal upon herself.

'If you're not careful, you're going to hurt yourself,' Brad Garwood frowned, releasing his hold and sitting her down in a chair so that he could examine the injured toe.

'I'll check my own injuries,' she snarled, pulling away from his touch and massaging the painful digit.

The heavy silence between them was suddenly interrupted by a loud knocking on the door. Hobbling into the hall, Sara discovered Steve on her threshold.

'Morning, Sis,' he greeted her with a quick peck on the cheek, then noticing her limp asked solicitously, 'Hurt your foot?'

'Stubbed my toe,' she replied shortly, retracing her steps to the living room with Steve close behind.

'On a piece of furniture?' he queried.

'It felt more like a brick wall,' she muttered.

Brad's expression hardened perceptibly when he saw Steve. 'I thought I made it clear that I didn't want you having anyone following me.'

'You did, and I'm not,' Steve replied, his eyes travelling from Sara to Brad and back again, while a frown began to form at the corners of his mouth. 'I came by to see my sister, and I have to admit I'm surprised to find you here.' The flavour of brotherly protectiveness in his manner was strong, causing Sara to cringe.

'I came by to apologise for the trouble I caused her last night and to offer her a job as my housekeeper,' Brad said nonchalantly.

'I was under the impression that that was a live-in position.' Steve's frown solidified.

'It is. However, I don't believe you have to worry. Cooking and cleaning don't seem to appeal to your sister.' Although Brad's tone was conversational for Steve's benefit, the covert glance he threw towards Sara carried the implication that it was his belief that she preferred not to work for a living. The hairs on the back of her neck bristled. If he had honestly been offering her a housekeeper's job, she might have considered the position. His manner, however, had implied something quite different. Of course, he had never actually stipulated anything other than cooking and cleaning in his job description, she reminded herself. It would serve him right if she took him at his word and accepted the position under the verbally stated conditions. Vengefully she pictured his surprise when he discovered that a housekeeper was all he had acquired.

'I should hope not!' Steve was saying, then turning his full attention on Sara, he demanded, 'I assume you're going to turn down the offer.'

'Actually, I haven't made up my mind yet,' she said, half out of rebellion towards Steve's domineering manner and half because she was not yet willing to give up her little fantasy. She would certainly like to teach the arrogant green-eyed male a lesson!

Brad's eyebrow raised slightly, but he said nothing.

'I've already talked to Helen,' Steve said sternly. 'She insists you come stay in the guest room until you can find a decent place to live.'

'That's impossible,' Sara firmly rejected this solution.

'You know I live on an erratic schedule. Trying to fit me into her life along with you and the children would be too much even for your very understanding wife. I like Helen too much to risk our friendship on a prolonged stay.'

'It isn't proper for a young woman to be living alone with an unmarried man. I won't allow it!'

'You won't allow it? I'm of age to make my own decisions,' she reminded him hotly.

'You may be over twenty-one, but I still feel responsible for you,' Steve threw back.

'I'm responsible for myself,' she snapped, coming very close to the end of her patience where male despotism was concerned. Catching the glint of sarcastic amusement in Brad's eye was the final straw. Rational thought gave way to revolt as she decided to teach both of them a lesson. 'And I've decided to accept Mr Garwood's offer of the housekeeping job.'

'Sara . . .' Steve's tone held a firm reprimand.

'I feel certain you have a desk waiting for you somewhere.' she interrupted, knowing that he was getting ready to launch a stout protest that might cost him his job. Taking him firmly by the arm, she led him to the door and unceremoniously shoved him out.

'Well, I'm not going to be the one to tell Mom,' he muttered as a parting shot. 'In fact I think I'll take Helen and the kids, and leave town for the week.'

'Coward!' she hissed back, closing the door after him, while internally quailing at the mere thought that Ida would ever get wind of this little charade.

Brad had followed her into the hall and was standing behind her. As soon as Steve was gone, he lifted her hair and kissed her neck. 'When do you want to move in?' he murmured against her skin.

Swinging out of his reach, she turned to face him, her

expression filled with fire. 'Tomorrow will be fine. But you'd better understand one thing—I'm to be your house-keeper and nothing more.'

His eyes narrowed dangerously as if he was preparing to challenge this stipulation.

'Just so we understand each other completely,' she continued acidly, 'I've always supported myself in a respectable manner and I intend to continue doing so. Until recently I had a teaching job, but because of budget cutbacks at the school where I worked, I lost the job at the end of last term. Since then I've been supplementing the money I earn from my art with my savings.'

'Why didn't you mention this before?' he growled. 'I would have thought that your experience last night would have taught you how dangerous playing games can be—or is playing games a way of life with you?'

'I didn't want to destroy your fun. You seemed to be enjoying the idea that I was promiscuous so very much,' she replied caustically, then with an acid smile added, 'Does this mean you're withdrawing your offer? Have you decided that you don't need someone to cook and clean for you?'

For a long moment they stood, two combatants at war with one another. It was Brad who broke the terse still-ness. 'No,' he said stiffly. 'Unlike you, I don't play games. I offered you the job and it's yours. I'll send some men and a truck over here tomorrow to move you. Since there's no room in my home for this furniture, I'll arrange to have it stored.'

'That won't be necessary,' she said tightly.

'Backing out?' he queried drily, a cynical smile curling one corner of his mouth.

That was exactly what she had planned to do, but the superior gleam in his eye clouded her reason. 'No,' she heard herself saying, 'it just won't be necessary to hire a truck. This place came fully furnished. I can move everything that's mine in a couple of trips with my car.'

'Fine!' Brad threw over his shoulder as he turned and slammed out the door.

Sara stood immobile. She knew she should run after him and tell him that she hadn't actually meant ever to move into his house, but her pride held her back. If she reneged now it would look as if she didn't have a sincere bone in her body.

The rest of the day she spent packing and arguing with herself. Late in the afternoon she took a load of paintings and a few sculptures over to the Grimes Gallery. Margarete Grimes had agreed to store them to save Sara the trouble of moving them around with her.

Margarete was a pleasant, middle-aged woman with an excellent head for business. Her husband was the artist in the family and in an effort to combine his skill with a steady income, they had opened a gallery several years earlier. It was through Margarete's skill as a saleswoman that they had met with great success. Having worked with the art community for so long, nothing shocked her, but she did raise an eyebrow when Sara gave her Brad's name and address and explained about her new position.

'It really is only a business relationship,' Sara explained, feeling the need to make this point perfectly clear.

'Of course, dear,' Margarete smiled, and Sara left feeling completely compromised.

That night, as she lay in her bed, the arguments continued to run through her mind, preventing sleep. She had to leave her present residence, and this job with Brad Garwood provided her with a place to live. She just couldn't move in with Steve and Helen. Besides, not only did the housekeeper's job provide her with an abode, it also paid enough that she could replenish her savings.

If only Brad Garwood could have been an elderly woman instead of such a disturbingly virile male! Arrogant, and ill-tempered, too, she added with a hostile grimace.

And how was she ever going to explain this situation to her mother? 'I'll tell her it's an honest living and that I'm getting paid for what women have done for free for years,' she muttered, pounding her pillow into a more comfortable shape. 'Well, I won't put it exactly that way,' she amended, closing her eyes and falling into a restless sleep.

# CHAPTER THREE

CRAWLING out of bed the next morning, Sara made herself a cup of coffee and reconsidered her position. Maybe it would work out all right if she moved in with Steve and Helen for a short time. She could help Helen with the housework and her brother and sister-in-law would have a live-in babysitter. Still, she hated to accept the solution. Steve was much too over-protective and her schedule simply did not coincide with that of Helen's and the children.

A knock on the door interrupted this mental debate. Answering it, she was startled to find Brad Garwood on her doorstep dressed in jeans and a pullover.

'I've come to help you move,' he announced, inviting himself inside, his manner coolly indulgent as if this was a necessary nuisance to be got out of the way with despatch. 'I couldn't get any work done, worrying about you falling down that ridiculous excuse for a staircase on the outside of this building. The thing should be condemned!'

This was her final chance to tell him she had changed her mind and was going to stay with Helen and Steve, but the words would not come.

Noticing her hesitation, he added blandly, 'The question is where do I move you to? Are you still planning to take me up on my offer, or have you changed your mind and decided to stay with your brother?'

'I would hope she's come to her senses and is coming to stay with Helen and me.' Steve joined them, walking in through the still opened door.

The word 'Yes' formed in her brain, but the word, 'No', came out. Shocked at her duplicity, she told herself it was a backlash reaction to Steve's domineering attitude. Noting that this was childish behaviour, she considered retracting her statement, then found herself arguing that she did need the money and couldn't possibly live under the same roof with her brother and still retain family harmony. Still, those reasons were not the final determining factor. The vague instinctive sensation that had kept her from backing out of her commitment to go to the ball now kept her from backing out of retaining the housekeeping job.

Brad's stoic acceptance of her decision did not surprise her. He was the kind of man who would honour his word, and he had offered her the job as accepted. What did surprise her was Steve's reaction. 'As long as I'm here, I might as well help with the move,' he frowned disapprovingly, but did not produce the heated argument she had expected.

'Life,' she muttered as she loaded several paintings into her car, 'can be very confusing!'

This conjecture was further strengthened on her arrival at Brad's home. It was a three-storey, red brick structure in the old section of Charleston, not much more than a mile from the Fallon residence. The buildings in this area had been renovated, retaining as much of their original outward appearance as was possible. They were mostly long, narrow structures which had originally been one room wide and three equally proportioned rooms in length. Today, of course, many of the interiors had been restyled to accommodate a more modern mode of living.

The narrow ends of these houses faced the street, giving them a sandwiched appearance. Having toured many of the older homes Sara knew that the reason they had been built in this sideways manner and in such tight proximity was that it had made it much easier for the early settlers to protect themselves against the frequent pirate attacks. The sturdy ends of the houses provided a man-made barricade, and the townspeople had only to block the narrow passages between their homes to complete their fortress.

To Sara's delight, Brad's home had a double-tiered piazza running the fully long length of the house. And as she parked behind him in the driveway, the sight of an elegant aged magnolia greeted her. Suddenly a sense of arriving at a place where she belonged swept over her.

'It's just the charm of this old residence which has greeted so many newcomers before,' she reasoned in an attempt to shake off the peculiar sensation, adding, 'and I've always loved piazzas and magnolias.' Still the impression lingered.

Walking through the back door behind Brad, she found herself in a large, spacious kitchen. An open door on her left revealed a bedroom, and it was in there that he placed her suitcases. The room was furnished in antique maple with handmade patchwork curtains and a matching quilted bedspread. The walls were white while the carpeting and woodwork were a pale yellow. If she had decorated it herself it couldn't have suited her better. 'I admire your decorator's taste,' she said, unable to hide her enthusiasm.

'It does suit you,' he murmured, regarding her curiously, then added stiffly, 'I chose the furnishings myself.'

'Then it's your taste I admire,' she rephrased her compliment, her manner taking on a stilted formality under his scrutiny.

Entering the kitchen loaded down with art supplies,

Steve interrupted the sudden heavy silence that had fallen between them. 'Where do these go?' he asked.

'Third floor, first door on your right,' Brad instructed, swinging abruptly around and going back out to his car for another load.

Unable to resist seeing the skylighted room as soon as possible, Sara also hurried out to her car and gathered up an armload of paintings.

'What this place needs is an elevator,' Steve complained when she caught up with him on the third floor landing.

Sara, however, did not respond as she passed him and walked into the promised studio. It was perfect. The skylight was large and centred, flooding the room with sunlight. The walls were white and the floor was a polished hardwood with an oval, braided area rug covering most of the surface. A couch and a small table were the only other furnishings, giving her plenty of room for her equipment and products.

Brad entered carrying her folded aluminium table which she used for her messier supplies.

'You ever consider putting in an elevator?' Steve demanded as the men unfolded the long table and set it up against one of the walls.

'After today I might,' Brad returned with a grimace, and the two men exchanged a comradely laugh.

Sara realised that this was the first time she had actually heard Brad Garwood laugh. In fact, it was the first time this morning that he had even smiled. In spite of the banter the two men had continually exchanged regarding the amount of art materials one woman could acquire, Brad had retained an air of indifferent reserve, especially in Sara's company. Considering the position in which she was placing herself this should have been reassuring, but instead his manner left her feeling disgruntled.

As the men started downstairs, she followed more slowly. It wasn't just the man's attitude which was distressing her. It was the house itself. Although she had never been here before, it felt comfortable, as if she had entered the home of a very dear friend. Being tense and overwrought she had expected to feel uneasy in the unfamiliar surroundings, but paradoxically, it was the lack of uneasiness which was making her apprehensive.

A couple of trips later, she was arranging the materials already brought up to her studio when Steve came in with an armload of items, followed by Brad with two sculptures.

'That's it,' her brother announced with an exaggerated sigh, then added as he paused to look around, 'I wonder if an artist lived here before. This room looks as if it was built for one.'

'I had the skylight put in,' said Brad, an indefinable edge to his voice. 'There's one in my workroom, too.'

'Why fix up two rooms with skylights?' Steve questioned.

'I was considering knocking out the adjoining wall to increase the size of my working space, but I just never got around to doing it,' Brad explained, dusting his hands off on his jeans, then hooking his thumbs in the pockets as he too surveyed the room.

Nodding to say that he understood how easy it was to put off large projects, Steve glanced at his watch. 'Speaking of work, I think it's time I got back to the office.' The glance he threw towards Brad suggested that he thought his boss should be leaving too.

'I'll be in a little later,' said Brad. 'I still have some work to finish up here.'

'Right, boss,' Steve replied with only a hint of a frown. Pausing by the door he added, 'I'm going to go ahead and assign two more men to The Pines' site.'

'Fine,' Brad agreed, a note of dismissal in his voice.

Because Steve was in charge of the security for all Brad's properties and projects, Sara knew that as private ventures the man had already built one large shopping mall plus an office complex. She also knew that The Pines, a townhouse community outside Charleston, was his newest independent project. The residences were all brick-fronted, styled to remind one of the Colonial period. There was a park with a lake in the northern corner and a large fenced playground in the centre, along with a small shopping area. It was well designed and the homes were being sold even before they were completed. Those that had been finished were already occupied. 'Are you having trouble at The Pines?' she asked, feeling suddenly very alone with the man now that Steve was gone.

'One of our caterpillars ended up in the lake last night. More than likely it was just a couple of kids out for a joyride. They probably scared themselves so badly they won't try anything else, but Steve thought it wouldn't hurt to add a little extra security for a couple of days.'

'He's a very cautious man,' Sara commented, her muscles beginning to tense as Brad continued to stand in the doorway watching her.

'I know. That's why I hired him. Sometimes, however . . .' he allowed the sentence to fade without completion as his features darkened momentarily, then regained their shuttered expression.

Feeling a desperate need to escape the man's scrutiny, Sara stood up and smoothed out her jeans. 'I don't know about you, but I'm starved. Since I'm now the cook and it's lunchtime, I'll go downstairs and see what I can find to whip up.'

'Make it sandwiches,' he directed. 'I have plenty of cold cuts and very little else.'

'All right,' she threw over her shoulder as she started down the stairs, only to discover he was following her.

'I've set up a household account,' he explained as she extracted the necessary ingredients from the refrigerator and set up the coffee pot. 'If you'll sign this card, I'll drop it off at the bank and you can start writing cheques today.'

Pausing momentarily, she did as requested. As she accepted the chequebook he handed her, their fingers touched, and she jerked away from the disturbingly fiery sensation. There was an intimacy about being alone in this house with this man she could not deny, and it caused her to have serious second thoughts about her present situation.

His mouth hardened into a tight line as he hooked his hands into his pants pockets and continued to watch her.

'What kind of sandwich would you like?' she asked, clearing her throat selfconsciously under his steady gaze.

'Ham and Swiss,' he returned curtly.

She considered apologising for her abrupt behaviour but what could she say that wouldn't be equally embarrassing. Choosing to pretend that nothing had happened, she continued preparing lunch. His eyes never shifted from her, and by the time she poured his coffee her nerves were near to breaking point. Picking up the plate with the sandwich, she carried it along with the coffee into the dining room and set them down on the table. For a moment Brad looked as if he was going to protest his ostracism from the kitchen table, then with an indulgently raised eyebrow he sat down.

'Do you want milk or sugar or both for your coffee?' she offered, her tone a stiff imitation of a stage-play maid.

'Neither,' he replied, matching her formal manner.

With a nod, she left. Back in the kitchen she made herself a sandwich, but when she tried to eat it, the thing tasted like cardboard. She did not understand what was happening to her, and this frightened her. Never had she been so suddenly or so keenly aware of a man. With Steve's departure, the reality of what she had got herself into was becoming more and more acute. The three-storey house was beginning to feel about as big as a doll's house. Angrily shoving the plate away, Sara chided herself for overreacting.

Brad Garwood's cool reserve should have convinced her that he had no designs on her. Then the thought that his attitude during the morning could have been an act for Steve's benefit suddenly popped into her mind. But Steve had been gone quite a while and Brad had continued to keep his distance. Who did she think she was anyway . . . a femme fatale? she grimaced into her coffee cup. The man had Monica Fallon to occupy him. Obviously he had momentarily considered a conquest on the side but was not willing to put any energy into it once he had been rejected. When this thought did not cheer her up, she frowned introspectively and began cleaning up the kitchen with the hope that physical labour would ease the confused tension building within her.

Hearing him go upstairs, she collected the plates from the dining room and completed straightening up the luncheon dishes, after which she considered spending the next hour in her bedroom unpacking to ensure that she missed him when he left the house. Then realising that she needed to ask him what he wanted for dinner and when he wanted to eat, she scolded herself again. After all, she was his housekeeper. There was no way she could perform her duties and totally avoid the man. 'If this was happening to anyone else, I'd say they had to be an idiot to have got themselves into this situation,' she muttered as she opened each cabinet and drawer in the kitchen, making a mental list of what was present before moving on to the refrigerator. 'And I'd probably laugh. Up until a week ago I considered myself a sane, rational person who only did minor dumb things. Now look at me!'

'I understand that talking to inanimate objects is not a serious condition until the objects start responding,' Brad's voice cut the air behind her.

Startled, Sara whirled around, a deep blush darkening her face. 'Have you been in here long?' she demanded.

'Only a moment. I'm not in the habit of eavesdropping, even on one-person discussions,' he replied coolly, continuing towards the door.

He had changed into a suit and she knew he was on his way to the office. Clearing her throat, she said, 'I need to know when you'll be wanting dinner.'

'Seven,' came his sharp businesslike response.

'And do you have any preferences?' she questioned.

Stopping with his hand on the door, he turned to face her. 'I'm sure whatever you prepare will be fine.'

'But . . .' she began to protest.

'You fix whatever you wish. I'll tell you when you have prepared something I dislike. Then we simply won't have that meal again,' he instructed, adding over his shoulder as he continued out the door, 'I assure you, however, that I'm a very easy man to please.'

Sara stiffened defensively as she watched the door swing closed. Then recalling his cool attitude towards her all morning, she chided herself for reading innuendoes into his words that weren't there.

After a trip to the grocery, she spent some time roaming around the house organising her work in such a way as to give herself the maximum amount of time to pursue her art. The arrangement of the house was simple. On the first floor was the kitchen, her bedroom with its private bath, an entrance hall and the dining room. On the second floor, as was traditional in these old homes, was the living room, or sitting room as it would have been referred to in times past. Then there was a combination library-billiard room and a guest bedroom plus a bath.

The third floor contained the master bedroom with its adjoining bath, her studio and Brad's workroom. Wandering into his bedroom, all done in greys, blues and whites, she again found herself questioning her judgment in taking this job. The man's presence was strong, creating an acute awareness within her of her own femininity.

Attempting to rid herself of the disturbing yet at the same time exciting sensation, Sara returned to the kitchen and started dinner, after which she reclimbed the stairs to her studio. Collapsing on the couch with her sketch pad, she paused to rub her sore leg muscles which were beginning to feel the strain of going up and down three flights of stairs on an almost continuous basis. Then attempting to ease the pain by reminding herself that this was great exercise for the heart, she opened her pad and began working. The idea she had been considering for her next painting, however, refused to materialise. In place of the tree-lined landscape she had meant to portray, a man's profile began to take form. Tearing off the first sheet, she threw it away and determinedly drew a tree, then right next to it again discovered herself redrawing the profile.

'It's no use,' she admitted to the empty room five sheets of paper later. 'I'm going to have to do his face.' Assuring herself that nothing more than an artistic urge was involved in this decision, she decided to use clay as her medium.

With the pot roast cooking slowly, she determined that she had plenty of time to run out and pick up the necessary materials. When she had an urge as strong as this, she knew it would only prolong the agony to put it off.

Carrying one of the heavy boxes of clay into the kitchen a little less than an hour later, she found Brad pouring himself a cup of coffee.

'I'll have your dinner on the table at seven as you requested,' she promised, nearly dropping the box of clay as she deposited it on the floor and hurriedly washing her hands before checking the roast in the oven. 'I had to run out to the art supply store for some material.'

'You've got to be kidding.' He shook his head in disbelief, leaning against the counter and watching her. 'After all that stuff we carried up this morning?'

Whenever the opportunity arose he watched her, and she wondered if this was his way of getting back at her for following him around at the ball. If so, it was working. She found it totally unnerving to have someone continually observing her as if she was a curiosity to be studied. 'It's clay,' she explained selfconsciously while carefully lifting the heavy pot containing the meat and vegetables from the oven. 'I don't normally keep it in stock.'

Placing the pot on top of the stove, she gathered up a place setting and went into the dining room. Brad joined her with a second.

'Are you expecting company?' she questioned innocent-ly.

'When we're the only two people in this house, it's ridiculous for us to eat at two different tables,' he replied arranging the setting at the place to his right.

'Did you eat with your other housekeepers?' she demanded, facing him squarely, determined to keep as much distance as possible between herself and this man.

'To be perfectly honest, you're the first housekeeper I've had.'

Her eyes widened. 'But you said . . .'

'I said the position was open,' Brad interjected before she could finish.

'But you implied that you'd had housekeepers before,' she glared.

'You obviously misinterpreted my words.' His manner was dry. 'I've always considered filling the position but have never taken the time to find a suitable person.'

Sara's back stiffened. 'Was it also a misunderstanding on my part when I thought you'd agreed that I was to be your housekeeper and only your housekeeper?'

'Sharing a meal is not the same thing as sharing a bed,' he pointed out, a note of exasperation in his voice implying that he found her behaviour exceedingly childish.

'You'd better understand right now that I have no intention of sharing anything with you, Mr Garwood,' she said, pronouncing each word distinctly as she fought to control her anger. 'We have a formal business arrangement, and that's the extent of our relationship.'

His expression darkened momentarily, then with an angry intake of breath he picked up the place setting and returned it to the kitchen.

'I'll carry this clay up to your studio,' he growled depositing the dishes on the counter and turning to leave. As he lifted the box a look of surprise came over his face. 'This is heavy. It's a wonder you didn't fall and break your neck carrying this kind of stuff up and down those rickety stairs at your apartment—or did you have help?'

'Since I left home, I've made it a point to carry my own

load,' she replied tightly, 'and I can take that clay upstairs myself.'

'I need the exercise,' he threw over his shoulder, and went out before she could insist on doing the job herself.

After dishing up the meat and vegetables on to a platter, she filled a plate for herself and then placed the platter on the dining room table along with a salad and a glass of iced tea. Brad had still not returned by the time the food was served and she was forced to go searching for him. She found him in the studio glancing through the sketches she had done during the afternoon.

'The profile looks familiar,' he noted with a touch of irony.

'I told you I found you . . . your face interesting,' she replied, adding tersely, 'in an artistic sense.'

For a moment he looked as if he was going to challenge her qualification, then a shuttered expression masked his features and his demeanour took on an air of indifference. 'I suppose you've come to tell me that dinner is ready.'

'Yes,' she confirmed, leaving the room and moving rapidly down the stairs.

Later, alone in the kitchen toying with the food on her plate, she admitted to herself that she should leave. But how could she without looking like some kind of a fool who couldn't decide from one minute to the next what she was going to do?

'You don't seem to be enjoying your cooking,' Brad's caustic tones broke into her contemplations. 'I thought it was rather good.'

'Thank you,' she murmured, accepting the offhanded compliment absently, still too engrossed in her own contemplation to care.

'I was wondering if there was any coffee,' he continued in the same hard voice.

'Yes, of course there is.' She pushed her chair back in preparation to rise, an embarrassed flush darkening her face. 'I was going to come in after a few minutes and ask if you wanted any. There's also dessert.'

'Fine, I'll take both,' he said, turning to leave the room, his manner that of the master of the house perturbed by his servant's less than attentive behaviour.

Sara knew he had a right to feel that way, especially after she had so determinedly demanded that their relationship be strictly formal. Still, the man made her angry. A small voice inside questioned if, perhaps, the anger was hiding another emotion, but she refused to listen. After setting the coffee and bakery-bought cake on the table in front of him, she walked over to the hutch and extracted a silver bell she had noticed earlier in the day. 'If you want anything just ring,' she instructed tightly, placing the bell near him.

'All Bogart ever had to do was whistle,' he noted drily.

'He was interested in satisfying a different kind of hunger,' she threw over her shoulder, making a hasty retreat before the exchange could turn into a confrontation.

Once back in the kitchen, her nerves were too taut to allow her to sit down. Running water into the sink, she began to scrub the pan in which she had cooked the roast while visions of her enigmatic employer flooded her mind. From one minute to the next, she could not decide whether to stay or grab her suitcases and run. Distracted, she dropped the pan as she started to dry it and the thing fell to the floor with a loud clatter.

Brad was in the kitchen immediately. 'Are you all right? What happened?' he demanded.

'I just dropped a pan,' she responded sharply, then

facing him icily she said, 'And I want to know what you're up to.'

'What I'm up to?' he questioned, his expression mock-innocence.

'You've been baiting me and I want to know why. If you want me out of this house all you have to do is say so. I thought I made it perfectly clear that I'm not the type of woman you thought I was.'

His expression hardened as he met the fury in her eyes. 'You're right, I have been baiting you,' he admitted, moving towards her as he spoke. 'You are presently presenting yourself as a very thoughtful, conservative young woman. Yet when I first encountered you, it was at a party which you'd gone to great lengths to crash, placing yourself in serious jeopardy of being arrested.'

'I told you Marc Fallon had brought me in,' she retorted, forced to lean her head backward to face him squarely as he came to a halt directly in front of her.

'And you think that alcoholic would have stood by you if his sister had discovered you and called the police?' he questioned contemptuously.

'He rescued me from her on the balcony and gave me a chance to escape,' she pointed out self-righteously.

'Granted,' he scowled, 'but it was a chance. He could have left you to her just as easily.'

Sara's expression wavered. 'All right, I admit it was a really dumb thing to do, but you saw how protective Steve is of me. When he came and asked me to do him that favour, I couldn't refuse. I was sure he had some strong rational reason for his concern.'

'And what exactly did he expect you to do in case there was any trouble?'

'I was only to leave and signal Sam if I saw anything suspicious.' She faced him defiantly.

Hooking his thumbs into the pockets of his pants, Brad stood staring down at her in cold indecision. 'Either you're a consummate actress or a total innocent.'

'I'm neither!'

Ignoring her protest, he continued in a threatening tone, 'First you let your brother talk you into a very dangerous game on a perfectly ludicrous hunch, and now you're sequestered alone in the home of a man who's propositioned you.'

'You agreed that I was only to be your housekeeper.' Outwardly she maintained an air of cool reserve while inwardly panic was beginning to build.

'I could have lied,' Brad pointed out, a satanic gleam sparking in his eyes. 'Surely you've heard the story of the big bad wolf who would go to any lengths to lure the lamb into his trap.'

'I thought even Yankees had an honourable streak in them somewhere,' she threw back as the colour drained from her face.

'Not all of them,' he muttered, breeching the distance between them.

Before she could take defensive action, Brad pinned her arms to her sides in his large hands. Wedged between his muscular form and the sink, Sara was trapped. Animal fear filled her eyes as she realised that to struggle would be useless against his superior strength. Her throat contracted in terror. Never had she seen a man so angry.

His face descended towards hers, stopping only inches from contact. While his green-black eyes held her captive, his breath stirred her hair when he spoke. 'Luckily for you, I do! Your brother is right to be protective towards you, woman. You do need a guardian!'

Panic gave way to rage. 'You . . . you . . .' she stammered, too infuriated to find the words to tell him what she thought of his behaviour.

His fingers deepened their impression in her flesh as his face moved even closer. Then just as his mouth brushed hers, he suddenly jerked back and drawing a sharp, hostile breath, released her and stalked out of the kitchen.

Standing rigidly, staring at the door as it swung closed, Sara was too furious to cry. He had no right to treat her like a child who needed constant supervision. Nor did she appreciate the manner in which he had chosen to teach her a lesson. Admittedly her behaviour the last couple of days had been less than prudent, maybe even a little irrational, but she didn't need him to point that out to her. She had Steve to perform that function.

After finishing the dishes, she carried the last of the clay up to her studio. Then, refusing to allow Brad to think she was sulking or afraid of him, she forced herself to face the man. Knocking first, she opened his workroom door.

'What do you want?' he growled, looking up from his drawing board. 'If it's an apology for my boorish behaviour, you have it. Although I find it totally unbelievable that someone as naïve as yourself could have survived this long alone.'

'I did not come in here for an apology or a further discussion of my naïveté,' she informed him coldly, maintaining a rigidly formal demeanour while fighting a strong urge to throw something at the arrogant male. 'I came in to ask if you'll be wanting some coffee this evening.'

For a long moment, Brad regarded her silently. Then slowly laying his pencil aside, he said, 'No, thank you. I have to run over to the complex. There's some paper work I have to catch up on before tomorrow. I apologise for leaving you alone on your first night in a strange house, but I won't be too late.'

'I'm not a child, Mr Garwood. I will not be frightened!' she glared, refraining from mentioning that the house did not feel strange to her at all. This fact was more distressing than comforting to her and she preferred to keep this knowledge to herself.

Brad left soon after. Too tired to even begin to work her clay, Sara unpacked her suitcases and after a quick phone call to Helen, went to bed.

# CHAPTER FOUR

BECAUSE Brad had not been home when Sara retired for the evening, she had not had an opportunity to speak to him about what time he wanted breakfast. However, being an early riser, she was certain she would be up before her employer. So, she was startled to be awakened by the sounds of someone opening and closing cabinets in the kitchen. Pulling on a robe, she went into the room to find Brad fully clothed in slacks and a pullover frowning down on her.

Running a hand through her unbrushed hair, she licked her lips nervously. 'I forgot to ask you what time you wanted breakfast,' she offered by way of an apology for being lax in her job. 'I'm usually up by five-thirty. It never occurred to me you would be up by five.'

'I've always preferred to work in the quiet morning hours,' he said, his frown being replaced by a shuttered expression. 'And I don't want breakfast right now. Six-thirty or seven will be fine. However, I do want some coffee. Where have you hidden it?'

'It's in the refrigerator,' she replied, covering a yawn with her hand. 'It stays fresher when stored at cooler temperatures.'

Throwing her an indulgent glance, he found the much sought-after can. 'Decaffeinated!' he muttered. 'A lot of good that's going to do when I have to stay awake at night.'

'Caffeine is bad for you. It makes you jittery and ruins your disposition,' she defended her choice. 'Don't you watch television?'

'Sometimes, but I don't let it determine my tastes,' he returned drily.

'Then I apologise for the coffee. I'll get you your caffeinated variety and you can continue to growl,' she threw back.

'I do not growl,' he snarled, turning to face her as she raised a sceptical eyebrow. 'However, since you bought this brand I suppose I can stand to drink it.'

As his eyes travelled over her, she suddenly became acutely aware of her less than proper appearance with her unbrushed hair, bare feet and hastily pulled on robe over nothing more substantial than a light nightgown. 'If you want to get back to your work, I'll finish making the coffee and bring you up a cup when it's ready,' she suggested.

'You're absolutely intriguing,' he muttered. 'Under the circumstances, any other woman would have made some remark regarding her appearance.'

'I'm perfectly aware of my appearance,' she informed him tightly, running a hand through her hair as she recalled the elegant Monica Fallon and guessed that the black-haired beauty would never allow a man to see her in anything less than complimentary conditions.

'I doubt that very much,' he frowned, then moving purposefully towards the door, he added, 'I would appreciate it if you would dress first before bringing my coffee up to me.'

'Yes, sir!' she hissed, infuriated that he should even consider the idea that she would go upstairs without dressing.

Back in her bedroom, Sara grimaced at the image in the mirror as she brushed her slightly longer than shoulder-length chestnut hair and tied it loosely back at the nape of her neck. Admittedly, her mouth was a little large, but she had always thought it balanced her slightly larger than normal brown eyes. Her cheekbones had a nice definition and her nose was straight. She was willing to concede that she was no raving beauty. Still, Brad didn't have to make her feel like such an ugly duckling.

'Well, at least, now that he knows what I look like in the morning, he won't be anxious to renew his efforts to get me into his bed,' she muttered, in an effort to cheer herself up. This thought, however, did nothing to alleviate the sting his remark had inflicted.

Delivering his coffee, she asked how he wanted his eggs, then went into her studio to work for a while before preparing breakfast. The man's presence permeated the air around her; a sensation she attributed to the fact that she was working on his bust. After building the mound of clay into approximate proportions in readiness for the actual shaping, she stepped back to survey her progress. 'Maybe I should add enough on top to carve out a pair of horns,' she mused sarcastically, then covering the clay she went downstairs to begin breakfast.

She had removed the bacon and was cracking the eggs into the skillet when Brad came into the kitchen carrying his place setting. 'I'm not a man who enjoys wasting time, nor do I live on a set schedule. So we'll eat breakfast together each morning and use this opportunity to map out our days so that neither of us interferes with the other's schedule.' When she started to protest, he held up his hand. 'You can consider it a business meal.' His manner made it clear that he intended to remain firm on this point.

'As you wish,' Sara conceded, unwilling to face another confrontation so early in the morning.

Her easy acquiescence obviously surprised him and he stood leaning against the counter watching her sceptically.

'Don't you have a paper to read?' she demanded, giving in to a fit of nerves.

'Sorry,' he apologised in a voice that held no remorse. 'I forgot how disturbing it can be to be constantly under surveillance.' Then a sudden tenseness filled the air as he added tersely, 'Tell me the truth. Is that why you're here?'

'What?' Pausing with the food-filled plates in her hands, Sara turned towards him, her face a mask of confusion.

'I half expected you to have changed your mind when I came by your place yesterday morning to help you move,' he elaborated. 'And it's now occurred to me that you might be here because Steve talked you into keeping an eye on me again.'

'He didn't, and I wouldn't have agreed to such an arrangement even if he had asked,' she assured him tightly, adding with a perplexed pout, 'Although I have to admit I was surprised by his acceptance of this situation. I expected him to try to talk me out of it when he showed up instead of helping me move.' Then as an afterthought she said, 'Besides, if he thought you were in any danger he wouldn't have allowed me near you.'

'He sent you to the ball,' he reminded her.

'Yes, but I was supposed to remain inconspicuous and have no contact with you.'

'You certainly botched that assignment,' Brad commented drily.

'That's why I'm an artist and not a detective,' she returned coolly, completing her action of placing the plates on the table.

As they began to eat, a heavy silence descended over the meal, in spite of Brad's earlier pronouncement that they would discuss their daily schedule. Sara forced herself to eat, refusing to give the man the satisfaction of knowing that he was upsetting her. Finally, though, unable to bear the strain any longer she said, 'You were going to outline your day for me so I could arrange my schedule.'

He had finished his eggs and was pouring himself a second cup of coffee. 'Since I'll be working here this morning, I'd like to have lunch around noon. A sandwich will suffice.'

'You're staying home?' she questioned disconcertedly.

'When I'm developing a new design I prefer to work at home. There are fewer interruptions,' he replied, watching her closely. 'But apparently this is going to interfere with your plans. Were you considering a whole-scale rearrangement of my workroom? If so, I should warn you that I don't allow anyone to touch the materials in there without permission. It may look like clutter to you, but I know every inch of that clutter and I don't want it shifted.'

'I understand about personal clutter,' she assured him. 'The reason I looked a bit dubious was that I'd planned to have a little company today.' She was about to explain that Helen was bringing her children over for Sara to babysit when Brad interrupted.

'A boy-friend?' he queried caustically, 'coming to check on your new living conditions?'

His manner raised her ire and without thinking, she said haughtily, 'As a matter of fact, yes, my very best boy-friend!'

'Then please don't change your plans on my account.' Pushing his chair back, Brad rose from the table. 'I would be interested in meeting the man. I'm curious to find out what type of male naïve lady artists fall for and what he thinks of your current situation.'

'I'll be certain to introduce you,' she snapped.

'Fine!' he threw over his shoulder as he left.

The minute he was gone, Sara regretted her deception.

This continual atmosphere of war between them had to come to an end. She knew it was mostly her fault. She was continuously overreacting to the man in the most childish way. He had good reason to question her judgment and her motives. She had met him under a lie, and considering her staunch conservative stand it did seem irrational that she should have placed herself in the present situation. She tried again to convince herself that it paid well and was an honest position, but considering the people involved, specifically a very virile male employer, the logic didn't hold; not if she considered the possible harm to her reputation.

However, right now, the how and why didn't matter; she needed to correct this present lie before it was too late. After all, she was the housekeeper and she should have asked his permission before making any plans.

Climbing the stairs, she found his workroom door open. He was standing in the windowed alcove gazing out on to the street below, his hands clasped behind his strong straight back.

'Excuse me,' she cleared her throat nervously.

'What is it, Sara?' he asked, turning to face her, his eyes green ice.

'It's about my company,' she began hesitantly, embarrassed to admit a lie in the face of his contempt.

'What about your expected visitor?' he questioned coldly. 'Are you afraid I might say something to this boy-friend of yours that will besmirch your character or give him the wrong idea?'

'No. I wanted to correct a misunderstanding. The person coming isn't a boy-friend in the sense you took it. He's my nephew . . . and my niece is coming, too. During the summer I watch them one day a week to give Helen a chance to run errands and do her shopping in peace. But

I'll cancel out for today. This is your home and I apologise for not checking with you first before telling Helen it would be all right.'

'Why didn't you explain all this downstairs?' Brad demanded.

Her mouth tightened into a hard line as her hope for a truce gave way to anger. 'I started to, but you interrupted.'

He stood rigidly regarding her as if weighing her defence, then his jaw relaxed and the ice left his eyes. 'I suppose I can be a bit overbearing,' he admitted gruffly. 'Guess I sounded like Steve.'

'A little,' she agreed, unable to totally hide her shock that he would shoulder some of the blame for the misunderstanding. 'But I shouldn't have overreacted. I'll call Helen and tell her not to bring the children over today.'

'No. They won't bother me,' he assured her, sitting down at his drawing board and picking up a pencil. 'In fact, I would like to meet them.'

'Of course,' she mumbled, still off balance from his sudden change of mood.

'And would you mind bringing me up a cup of coffee?' he requested as he swung a straight edge into place and began to draw.

'Yes, sir,' she replied, leaving the room to comply with his wish. While pouring the coffee and carrying it upstairs, she frowned at herself. She had her truce, so why did she feel disgruntled? Brad's reference to sounding like Steve played over and over in her mind. Obviously he had totally given up the idea of seducing her, probably after this morning's exposure to her appearance, and now saw himself in the role of a big brother protecting an incredibly naïve kid sister. Well, she wasn't so naïve as he thought just a little confused lately, and she didn't need another big brother. Steve filled that role more than adequately.

When Helen came by to drop off the children, her bright blue eyes were filled with curiosity. 'Steve's not pleased with this arrangement, but he doesn't seem to be as adamantly against it as I thought he would be,' she said, walking into Sara's bedroom and bath for a quick inspection. 'This is really nice. Much better than that apartment you were in with those awful outside stairs.'

'True,' Sara agreed, smiling at the slightly plump blonde who continued to rattle on without pausing for a breath.

'And when I get back, I want a complete tour, but right now I have to rush. As usual I'm running late. I never used to be late all the time, but for some reason I've never been able to get my act together since Joanie was born. Don't let anyone tell you that the second one is only half as much trouble as the first!' She finished with a quick kiss on each of the children's cheeks and one for Sara, then with a wave was out the back door in a flurry, her car keys jangling in her hand.

'Have a nice day,' Sara called after her from the doorway.

'Be back around three,' Helen shouted back and with a second quick wave drove off.

'What are we going to do today?' Tommy demanded excitedly as soon as his mother was gone and his aunt's attention could be devoted entirely to himself and his sister.

Sara smiled down at her nine-year-old nephew, so like his father with his brown hair and brown eyes, and his seven-year-old fair-haired, blue-eyed sister who was almost an exact replica of her mother. 'I thought you two could make kites while I do some sculpting,' she replied, leading them up the stairs to her studio.

'Excellent!' Tommy exclaimed, using the latest word that had replaced 'terrific' in his youthful vocabulary.

'Yes, excellent!' Joanie copied her brother.

The door of Brad's workroom was open and as they reached the landing, he came out to meet them. 'What's so excellent?' he smiled. It was a warm open smile that caught Sara completely off guard as she realised how very charming the man could be when he chose to show that side of himself.

'We're going to make kites,' Joanie informed him, her cheeks pink with pleasure.

'This is my niece Joanie and my nephew Tommy,' Sara introduced her charges. 'And children, this is Mr Garwood.'

Tommy had been standing silently studying Brad, his demeanour not unlike that of his father's when Steve found himself in a new situation of which he did not totally approve. As Sara finished and he reached out to accept Brad's proffered handshake, his expression became pronouncedly critical. 'So you're the man my aunt is living with,' he frowned.

Sara flushed scarlet. 'I'm not living with Mr Garwood,' she corrected.

'You told Mother that the room downstairs was your bedroom,' he reminded her.

'I'm living in Mr Garwood's home, but I'm not living with Mr Garwood,' she struggled with what was obviously a losing battle.

'Does that mean that the two of you are married?' Joanie asked, her mouth forming a pout. 'You promised I could be in your wedding when you got married.'

'I've already told you that they're not married.' Tommy turned towards his sister, his voice expressing his exasperation with her single-minded concern. 'That's why no one wants to be the one to tell Grandma Ida.'

It was apparent that the children had overheard their parents discussing this situation. Still flushing, Sara met Brad's gaze. 'I suppose you find this amusing,' she accused.

'Perhaps a little,' he admitted, a slightly sardonic gleam in his eyes.

'What's "amusing" mean?' Joanie asked her brother as she watched the exchange between the adults with interest.

'Funny,' he whispered back.

'Funny?' she mused, then with that angelic look of wisdom only children can achieve, announced loudly, 'No one is going to think it's *amusing* when Grandma finds out.'

'Why don't we forget about Grandma and go make your kites?' Sara suggested, taking both children by the hand and dragging them down the hall, followed by a pair of thoughtful green eyes.

Later, as she attempted to mould the clay into the correct form, Sara was forced to admit that children had a way of making a point more clearly than any adult argument. No matter how properly she behaved, the majority of people were going to believe that she and Brad Garwood were having an affair.

Only halfway able to concentrate on her work, she was having a great deal of difficulty getting the head proportioned correctly, which did not help to soothe her taut nerves.

'Here he is,' Tommy announced, startling her out of her contemplation as he re-entered the studio holding on to Brad's hand.

She had noticed him leave, but had assumed he had gone to the bathroom. 'What?' she questioned in some confusion.

'You were muttering about how you couldn't get the head right without Mr Garwood, so I went and got him for you,' the child explained matter-of-factly, adding, 'Is he an artist too?'

'He's the model,' she replied, the flush returning to her face. 'But you shouldn't have bothered him.'

'You did say you needed him,' Joanie came to her brother's defence. Then as if she felt it was necessary to explain her aunt's eccentricities, the little girl smiled up at Brad and said, 'Aunt Sara always mutters to herself when she has a problem. She says it comes from living alone and having only herself to talk to. Tommy and I always try to help when we're around.'

'I knew I should have cancelled today,' Sara frowned.

'Only God can cancel a day,' Tommy mimicked one of his mother's favourite sayings.

'How can I help?' Brad cut into the exchange, indicating with a nod of his head that the boy should return to his kite building. Surprisingly the child obeyed.

'I'm sorry Tommy disturbed you,' Sara apologised, still feeling flustered.

'I was going to take a break anyway.' His voice held an indulgent note. 'What can I do to help?'

Knowing that a refusal of his offer at this point would only make her look even more foolish and admitting that she honestly did need the man to model, she moved a stool near to where she was working. 'You could sit here for a few minutes.'

'The last time she asked me to sit for a few minutes, it was ten hours,' Tommy commented in a consoling voice.

'It was less than an hour, and you never stopped squirming,' Sara corrected, throwing the boy a lopsided grimace.

'It was at least two hours, and I sat perfectly still

without even hardly breathing for a whole ten minutes once,' he rebutted.

'It was one hour, and you sat perfectly still for a whole four minutes once,' she conceded, adding playfully, 'I considered renaming the piece "Child in Action" and adding a few extra arms and legs.'

'Oh, Aunt Sara!' the boy grinned sheepishly before returning to his cutting and pasting. His bright eyes indicated that he enjoyed this light bantering with his aunt.

'You're very good with children,' Brad remarked as Sara positioned him.

'Thank you,' she smiled tightly, having a difficult time fighting the fiery sensation in the tips of her fingers as she moved his head slightly to one side.

'Mom says she should have some of her own,' Joanie offered happily, glancing up from her work. 'But she'd have to get married first so I could be in the wedding.'

'Yes, and Dad says if she was married he wouldn't have to worry about her living alone. Of course, she's not living alone now, but he still seems to be worried.' Tommy contributed his two cents.

'You two are a couple of walking, talking encyclo-paedias today,' Sara interjected before either child could continue the discourse on how the family felt about her current lifestyle and their plans for her future. 'Why don't you close your covers for a while and concentrate on your kites?'

'Yes, ma'am,' Tommy replied, catching the warning look in his aunt's eyes and throwing his sister a cautionary glance.

For the next half hour the room was quiet except for the short exchanges between the children concerning their kite building. Brad sat stiffly while Sara glanced back and forth between him and her clay, sometimes pausing to move completely around him. His was a strong face, and yet when his eyes fell on the children there was a perceptible softening. She found herself staring more than working and had to mentally admonish herself more than once.

'Tommy's right,' Brad broke his silence at the end of thirty minutes. 'It does seem like ten years.'

'You can move if you like.' She bit her lip selfconsciously. 'I've got a good enough start to go on without you if you want to go back to your own work.'

He rose and stretched but did not immediately leave. Instead, he wandered over to see what kind of progress the children were making on their project. 'Where do you plan to take them to try out their kites once they're finished?' he asked, returning his attention to Sara as she attempted to size the nose properly.

'I hadn't thought about it,' she replied, finding the vivid green of his eyes made them so predominant that it was difficult to proportion the face properly. 'I guess I was actually planning to leave that part of the project up to Steve.'

'I have to run out to The Pines for a while. If you'd be willing to pack a picnic lunch, there's a large open space in the park out there they could use,' he offered.

Sara's first inclination was to decline, but both Tommy and Joanie immediately jumped up and began pleading with her to accept.

Thus it was that a little over an hour later, she sat on a blanket across the remains of a picnic lunch from Brad Garwood watching her niece and nephew running back and forth in an attempt to launch their more colourful than functional creations. An ancient live oak, its trunk so wide, four children could have hidden undetected behind it and its foot-thick branches, decorated with pale thready masses of Spanish moss swaying gently in the breeze, provided a comfortable shade for the adults.

Normally this soft environment would have produced an air of peace within her, but the presence of the man only a few feet away caused her to remain tense. Feeling a strong need to break the silence between them, she asked, 'Do you come out here often for picnics?'

'No. In fact, this is the first picnic I've been on in years. I guess I have a tendency to let my work take over my life.' Brad was watching the children and there was a musing quality in his voice when he spoke.

Sara knew from various snatches of conversations in which Steve had mentioned their mutual employer that Brad had come from a poor family and had worked hard to build the life he had today. He had paid his own way through school doing manual labour and then sent his brother and sister through. 'That's not an uncommon fault,' she commented quietly.

The breeze caught her hair and sent a strand over her face. Reaching across the distance between them, Brad brushed it back behind her ear. For a second her heart seemed to stand still as their eyes met and his hand traced the line of her jaw in a caress that ignited a fiery glow over her entire body. Then abruptly he broke the contact and in the same motion lifted his tall frame from the blanket. 'I did come out here to check on a few matters,' he announced briskly. 'I'll be back to take you and the children home in a little while.'

Before she could speak he was moving away. Watching him stride across the grass to the street, Sara realised her hands were shaking and chided herself for allowing the man to elicit so strong a reaction from her. After all, she hardly knew him, and what she did know was not particularly favourable. He was overbearing and arrogant. Still

. . . Her hand went up to touch her jaw where the imprint of his fingers continued to linger.

'He thinks I'm naïve and childish, and I'm beginning to think he's right!' she muttered angrily, quickly gathering up the remains of the picnic before joining Tommy and Joanie in their attempts to get their kites off the ground.

When they returned to town, Brad paused at the house only long enough to drop Sara and the children off. Then, informing her that he would require dinner at seven, he left for his office. She greeted his departure with a sigh of relief. Helen was due back soon, and although Sara was fond of her sister-in-law, the woman could be even more blunt than the children.

And as Sara suspected, Helen intended to be blunt about her feelings regarding the present situation. 'It's a beautiful house,' she said as they returned to the kitchen after a full inspection of the premises. 'Although I don't know how you can stand running up and down three flights of stairs all day long.'

'It's supposed to be healthy.' Sara smiled apprehensively. She knew her sister-in-law well enough to know when Helen was preparing to be frank.

'You know that I understand how over-protective Steve is with you and how much it gets on your nerves,' Helen began, her face and tone taking on a certain motherly quality which had become more and more pronounced over the years thanks to the practice she was receiving from communicating with her own children. 'However, in this case I think he has a point—or had a point, I should say, since he seems to have reconciled himself to this situation much better than I would have ever dreamed was possible. Anyway, I've met Brad Garwood and he's quite a man. Living here alone with him is sure to cause gossip. There are going to be people who'll never believe that your relationship is strictly business. And, if nothing else, you should consider Ida's reaction. She'll never forgive any of us.'

'I know,' Sara admitted.

'You can move in with us,' Helen finished.

'I don't think that will be necessary, but thanks anyway,' Sara refused. 'I'm sure I can find a place for myself, and I promise I'll start looking right away.'

'Just keep in mind that once gossip starts it's harder to get rid of than weeds,' Helen warned. 'Every time you think you've eradicated the whole lot, a new batch pops up somewhere else.'

'I'll remember,' Sara promised.

After Helen and the children had left, she started dinner, then wandered aimlessly around the house. She knew her sister-in-law was right. She had known almost from the beginning that she could not remain under Brad Garwood's roof. Still, she was filled with a deep regret coupled with what could only be described as a sense of foreboding. 'I'm being ridiculous,' she muttered, gazing out the second floor window of the living room. 'I'm just overwrought. Ever since the ball, I haven't been myself. If I had been myself I would never have moved in here in the first place.'

'You're muttering to yourself again,' Brad startled her as he entered the room. 'What's the problem this time?'

'I wasn't mut . . .' Whirling jerkedly around, Sara started to deny the accusation, then stopped herself. 'Yes, I was muttering. I can't stay here. It was foolish of me to agree to be your housekeeper. Steve's made me angry and I wanted to teach the both of you a lesson.' Although Brad raised an eyebrow at this confession, he continued to remain silent. 'Anyway,' she hurried on, 'I'm not as liberated as I thought, and I hadn't honestly considered all the consequences.'

Expecting a sarcastic response, she was surprised when he merely nodded in thoughtful agreement. 'When do you want to leave?'

As she realised that he was no doubt anxious to be rid of her now that he knew she was not going to submit to having an affair, her back straightened. 'I can move in with Helen and Steve tomorrow.'

'I'm not anxious to be rid of you, Sara,' he frowned as if reading her mind. 'I only want you to do what you feel is right for you.'

The hint of brotherly concern was back in his voice. 'Fine,' she muttered through clenched teeth, feeling irrationally irritated as she brushed past him and went downstairs to finish dinner.

For the rest of the evening, other than the times when she was serving the meal, she avoided his company. She didn't understand why she was reacting so childishly, but for some reason she couldn't seem to help herself. Therefore, to avoid embarrassment, she avoided him. This behaviour did not go unnoticed, and an air of tension built to a density so thick it could be cut with a knife.

The phone rang around nine. Sara started to answer it, but when it stopped in the middle of the second ring she knew Brad had picked it up. Returning her attention to the clay in front of her, she frowned. She could not dissociate the man from the sculpture, and the emotional battle raging within her was dramatically affecting her creativity.

Suddenly a knock sounded on the studio door, followed by the structure being thrust open. 'That call was from one of the residents at The Pines,' Brad said tersely, remaining in the doorway. 'She was pretty hysterical, but from what I could gather, she saw some kids sneaking into an unfinished unit near hers. I've alerted security and I'm going out there myself. I want you to call Steve and tell him to meet me there.'

'Of course,' Sara replied coolly, but as he started to leave she heard herself add in an anxious tone, 'Be careful.' Why she had said it, she did not know, and her face flushed red as he paused to give her a searching look.

Averting her head, she brushed past him to pick up the phone in the hall and began dialling Steve's number. But as he started down the stairs, her head turned towards him of its own volition and, as if he felt her eyes on him, he met her concerned gaze. 'I'll be back soon,' he promised.

After calling Steve and relaying the message, Sara returned to her studio, but she could not work. Covering the clay, she paced nervously around the house. She did not know why she felt apprehensive, but there was no denying that she did. If she was a person who believed in premonitions she would have thought that was what she was having—a premonition of disaster, and it involved Brad.

It was nearly midnight when a car finally pulled into the drive. Running upstairs to her studio, she uncovered her clay. It was her intention to pretend that she had been so engrossed in her work, she had lost track of the time. She certainly did not want Brad knowing she had been anxiously waiting up for him.

Hearing Steve's voice, she walked out to the landing and looking downward was greeted by a sight that caused her breath to catch in her throat. Her brother was accompanying a bloodied, bandaged Brad up the stairs.

'What happened?' she managed to choke out, taking in the slight swelling under each of the two white patches on his face and the securely wrapped wrist suspended in a sling.

'Seems some idiot in a truck drove out of a dirt side road right in front of Brad,' Steve explained as they reached her.

'I swerved to miss him and went into a ravine,' Brad finished, his voice sounding slurred.

'The doctor gave him something for the pain,' Steve explained in answer to Sara's questioning glance. 'I'm going to put him to bed.'

'Shouldn't he be in hospital?' she suggested, fighting a strong urge to wrap her arms around the injured man and hold him tightly to her.

'Yes,' Steve frowned.

'No,' Brad growled.

Throwing Sara a 'there's nothing I can do to change his mind' look, Steve said, 'After I get him tucked in, I'll need some ice packs for his wrist.'

'I'll fix them right now,' she threw over her shoulder, already on her way down the stairs. In the kitchen, her hands shook as she emptied ice trays into plastic bags. She had known something terrible was going to happen to Brad, but how?

Back upstairs, she waited impatiently outside the bedroom door until Steve opened it. Refusing to give him the ice bags, she approached the bed herself to discover Brad already asleep, his face pale and drawn. Carefully she arranged the ice around his wrist, then picked up the prescription bottle on the night table next to the bed.

'The doctor sent those along for the pain,' Steve explained in hushed tones.

Replacing the bottle on the table, she took her brother's arm and led him out of the room. Then closing the door securely behind her, she demanded, 'Just how badly is he hurt?'

'Not really badly,' he assured her. 'He has a few stitches

under those bandages and his wrist is badly sprained, but he got off easy. You should see the car!'

'I'd rather not,' she returned tightly. 'What happened to the other driver?'

'Nothing. Whoever it was took off. Didn't even stop to help.' Steve shook his head angrily. 'It was probably a bunch of drunken kids. They use those old side roads for their drinking parties.'

'Probably,' she muttered softly, her uneasiness still strong. Then as an afterthought she asked, 'Where did it happen?'

'Just south of The Pines. I got there about the same time as the ambulance.' Steve had started down the stairs and Sara followed. 'Now why don't you make me some coffee while I call Helen and tell her what's happened and that I won't be home tonight.'

'Are you going back out to The Pines?' she questioned.

'No, I'm staying here.' A strong air of brotherly protectiveness accompanied this statement.

'There's no reason for you to stay,' she frowned. 'I'm perfectly capable of taking care of Brad Garwood.'

'It's not proper for you to be running in and out of his bedroom.'

Throwing him an exasperated glance, she said, 'With Brad in his condition, I'm sure I'll be perfectly safe.'

'What about when he wasn't incapacitated?' Steve's tone was deadly serious.

She was tempted to tell him that it was none of his business, then realising that such a remark would only lead to an unproductive confrontation, she said, 'He treats me as if he's my big brother, and frankly, having two such specimens of that nature in my life is a little more than I care to handle.'

Visibly relaxing, Steve smiled up at her. 'He also told

me that you'd decided to move out tomorrow. Said you were concerned about your reputation. I'm glad you finally came to your senses.'

'I was going to,' Sara admitted with a sigh, 'but I can't now. He'll need someone to look after him for the next couple of days. Besides, that will give me time to find a place of my own. I don't relish moving in with you and Helen and then into another place. Three moves in two weeks is more than I care to face.'

'So he really treats you like a big brother,' he mused, then added grudgingly, 'Well, I guess it's okay as long as you're out of here by the time Mom returns.'

'It's amazing how a five-foot, ninety-eight-pound, grey-haired female can cower a big strapping six-foot-two-inch man like yourself,' Sara chided mischievously, relieved that he wasn't going to launch into the long-overdue protest. She was too anxious about the man upstairs to have handled an argument with finesse.

'Don't try to tell me you aren't intimidated by her,' Steve defended himself.

'No, but I'm closer to her size and she has me greatly beaten in age.'

'Just promise me you'll be out of here by the time she hits town,' Steve's manner became serious once again.

'I promise,' she said, knowing that he was more concerned about her than their mother. Steve had always been able to handle Ida, though he would never admit it. Then recalling the reason that Brad had gone out in the first place, she asked, 'What about the vandals? Did you catch them?'

'No,' he shook his head, his jaw hardening in anger. 'I never made it to The Pines. When I discovered Brad was in the accident I followed the ambulance to the hospital and stayed with him. But I did call my men from there.

They said they checked all the units right after Brad's call but didn't find anything. Whoever it was must have been scared off. Probably saw the woman watching them and left.'

'I wonder why she didn't call the security men right there. Surely you gave their number to all the residents?' Sara frowned.

'Maybe she did and no one was near the phone. It's not supposed to happen, but it does.'

'I suppose so,' she muttered, not looking completely convinced.

'What's bugging you, Sis?' Steve probed, picking up on her mood.

'I don't know.' Sara pursed her lips in an attitude of self-ridicule. 'I think its just me. My nerves have been a little on edge lately.'

'It's probably Mom,' he teased. 'Ever since we were kids she's had us psyched out. She always seemed to know when we were in trouble or formulating some mischief. I'll bet that in your subconscious, you half expect her to burst through the door any minute and read you the riot act for getting into this situation.'

'I had some help, remember,' she reminded him with a playful grimace. Still, he had hit a nerve. Once when she was around eight years old, she had ridden her bike into the woods without permission and had fallen and broken her ankle. She had been terrified that no one would find her, but her mother had shown up right away. 'I heard you calling me,' Ida had said, and at the time Sara had accepted that answer. Later, when she was older, she had remembered the incident and realised that her voice could not possibly have carried all the way from the woods to the house. When she had questioned her mother, Ida had explained that it was a gift she had inherited from her mother and Sara would have it too. 'You'll always know when someone you love is in danger,' Ida had told her as if this was a truth carved in stone.

Admittedly, through the years, Sara had always known when Steve was hurt, and then there was the time Joanie had broken her leg. Sara had known something was wrong with the child before anyone called her. Or the time Tommy had stitches or when Helen had burned her hand. Still . . . Brad Garwood? 'Ridiculous,' she muttered.

'What's ridiculous?' Steve asked, reminding her of his presence.

'It's ridiculous that you're still here and not at home with your wife and children,' she said, taking him by the arm and leading him to the door.

''night, Sis.' He gave her a quick kiss on the cheek, while studying her dubiously. 'You call me if you need any help.'

'I'm sure I can manage,' she stated briskly, shoving him outside and waving him on his way.

'Brad should have another one of those pain pills in ten minutes,' he called back as he climbed into his car.

Waving to say she had heard, Sara closed the door and started back upstairs. Stopping before she reached the first landing, she returned to the kitchen to make a couple of fresh ice bags to take with her.

A few minutes later when she went into Brad's bedroom, he appeared to still be asleep, but the moment she approached the bed, his eyes opened.

'I'm sorry if I woke you,' she apologised, her voice sounding much calmer than she felt as a sense of intimacy permeated the room.

'Where's Steve?' he scowled.

'I sent him home to his wife and children,' she replied matter-of-factly, refusing to be intimidated. 'I may not be an expert on first aid, but I can give you a couple of pills and arrange ice packs.'

'What about the vandals?'

'They left without doing any damage,' she told him coolly. 'And now it's time for you to have a pill, then I'm going to change the ice bags.'

As he levered himself up on his good arm, the sheet fell away from his chest exposing an expanse of tanned muscular flesh. Retrieving the covering, he pulled it back up around himself.

'I am an artist. I have seen the male torso before,' Sara chided, though she had to admit that this particular male torso stimulated a curiously exciting reaction within her which had not been engendered by any of the other male bodies to which she had been exposed.

'Let's just say that I'm the modest type,' Brad muttered, taking the pill from her and washing it down with a drink of water. 'Now you go to bed like a good girl and let me get some rest.'

'After I change the ice bags on your wrist,' she stipulated. From the linen closet she extracted a hand towel and after replacing the old ice packs with the new, wrapped the ice-encased wrist in the towel. 'I'm sorry if this hurts,' she said, catching a glimpse of the pain in his eyes.

'Just finish,' he requested tightly.

Biting her lip, she fought back a strong urge to kiss the swollen wrist, just like her grandmother and mother had always kissed her childhood injures 'to make them better'. Then chiding herself for the foolish notion, she asked, 'Do you have any safety pins or large rubber bands?'

'Rubber bands in the desk in my workroom,' Brad answered shortly.

Returning a couple of minutes later with two large rubber bands, Sara slid them over the towel to hold it and the ice in place. 'How does that feel? Is it too tight?' she questioned anxiously as his jaw hardened against the pain.

'It feels fine. Now will you please go to bed,' he requested.

'I'm only trying to be helpful,' she snapped, giving in to the anger that was building inside her in response to his obvious dislike of having her nurse him.

'And I appreciate your help, but I do want to get some rest.' His manner was less hostile coupled with an increasing drowsiness.

Sara regretted letting her temper get the better of her again. The man was injured and in pain. It was only natural that he would be irritable. 'I know,' she said softly, letting her voice say she was sorry for her fit of temper. 'I'll be going now.'

He was already nearly asleep, and she guessed that the effect of the pill would last until morning. The bottle had cautioned the user not to take more than one every six hours.

Back in her own room, she changed into her nightgown and crawled into bed, but sleep would not come. She kept thinking about her premonition and what her mother had said. Finally, giving in to an uncontrollable urge, she left her bed and after pulling on a robe went upstairs and entered Brad's bedroom. Walking stealthily over to the bed, she gazed down on his sleep-relaxed features. The velvet softness of his eyes when he had held her following her near-fall and her extremely erotic physical reaction to his touch haunted her. Then she again recalled the ice in those same eyes when he had accused her of lying and the arrogance in his manner when he had propositioned her. 'It just can't be true,' she muttered, turning away and quickly fleeing the room. 'It just can't be. I can't be in love with Brad Garwood!'

# CHAPTER FIVE

IT WAS early the next morning when the loud clatter of falling metal brought Sara out of the realm of dark dreams and into a groggy state of consciousness. Pulling on her robe, she stumbled out into the kitchen to find Brad shirtless, clothed only in a pair of slacks, attempting to make coffee. He had obviously overcome his embarrassment, and suddenly she wished he hadn't, as the desire to touch the smooth hard muscles of his back assailed her.

'I didn't have a firm enough grip and the can slipped. Sorry I woke you,' he apologised as he picked up the fallen container and placed it between his arm and body while again attempting to prise off the lid. Because he was right-handed and because the injured wrist was the right one, he was operating under a handicap.

'I'll finish that,' Sara insisted tightly, belting her robe and taking the coffee from him. Then, noticing his naked, swollen wrist, she plopped the can on the counter and glared up at him. 'Where's your bandage?'

'I took it off to shower and couldn't get it wrapped right,' he replied, a touch of sheepishness in his expression.

'Men!' she muttered, fighting the tender chord his almost boyish response struck. Then, abandoning the coffee making, she ran upstairs to retrieve the long piece of elastic. When she returned, Brad was measuring the coffee into the pot. 'I said I'd do that,' she scowled.

'I might as well work out a system now since I'll have to do it for myself tonight,' he threw over his shoulder.

'No, you won't. I'm going to stay a while longer.'

This announcement of her intentions brought a sudden guardedness to his features as he turned to face her. 'There's no reason for you to change your plans on my account,' he frowned. 'I'm perfectly capable of taking care of myself.'

Her pride wanted her to pack immediately and be on her way, but she could not bring herself to leave him in his present condition. A stronger force than pride would not allow a desertion. 'No, you aren't,' she said stiffly. 'Besides, I don't relish moving three times in rapid succession. Staying here a couple of extra days will give me a chance to find a place of my own and I won't have to move in with Helen and Steve and then move again.'

'I suppose, under the circumstances, that would be the most practical solution for both of us,' he conceded grudgingly.

Unsuccessfully attempting to ignore the pain his less than agreeable attitude was causing, Sara indicated a chair at the kitchen table. 'If you'll please sit down, I'll re-wrap your wrist.'

'I didn't mean to sound so out of sorts,' he apologised tightly as he followed her instructions. 'I do appreciate your concern.'

Her jaw tightened at the hint of indulgence in his voice. 'I don't want to be a nuisance.'

'You're not a nuisance,' he growled softly, then drew a sudden sharp breath of pain as she began manoeuvring the bandage around the swollen joint and hand.

'Are you certain this isn't broken?' she questioned, feeling his pain as if it was her own.

'The doctor said it wasn't, and he should know. He took enough X-rays.'

Although Brad did not complain, Sara read the pain in

his eyes and when she finished, said, 'I'll go upstairs and get you one of those pain pills.'

'No!' he rejected the offer forcefully. 'They make me feel groggy.'

'You look tired. You should go back to bed,' she suggested, all the time wanting to reach out and touch his drawn features.

'The cleaning service comes today,' he scowled. 'And I have work to do.'

'You don't plan to go into the office?' she demanded incredulously.

'Why not? Do you think I'll frighten my secretary?' His hand went up to touch the edge of the bluish swelling surrounding one of the two lines of stitches on his face.

'I think you should stay at home and rest.' Her voice took on a softly coaxing quality. 'I know your wrist is still throbbing. You won't be able to get any work done and you should keep ice on it all day today.'

'You're probably right,' he grimaced, exercising the fingers of the affected hand with obvious difficulty.

'Of course I am,' she affirmed, adding over her shoulder as she moved swiftly towards her bedroom, 'I'm going to dress and then fix breakfast while you go back to bed.'

However, later as she was cracking eggs into the skillet, Brad came back into the kitchen fully clothed. 'I agreed to stay at home and keep my wrist in an ice pack. I did not agree to play the role of an invalid,' he informed her in response to her critical glance.

'I suppose that's as good a compromise as I can hope for from a bull-headed male,' she muttered, filling two fresh ice bags for his wrist and using the oversized rubber bands to hold them in place once again.

'Bull-headed?' he grumbled. 'If I'd known I was going to get no sympathy here I would never have agreed to stay. At least my secretary would have had a kind word for me.'

Suddenly worried that he might change his mind, Sara tenderly touched his slightly swollen skin. 'I'm sorry you were hurt, and I apologise for calling you bull-headed.'

'You do know how to get your way, don't you?' he murmured, his expression darkening as he turned away, breaking the contact.

With his back towards her, he poured himself a cup of coffee while Sara stood for a long moment staring selfconsciously at her hand. Then with a rigid posture, she forced herself back into motion and finished putting the breakfast on the table. Obviously Brad did not want her to touch him. She would be certain not to make the same mistake twice.

At precisely eight, the cleaning service crew arrived, and Brad introduced Sara as his temporary housekeeper and artist in residence.

'You Yankees have a marked sense of humour,' the head of the crew, a woman named Kate, laughed good-naturedly. 'And I've always suspected there was a bit of the Irish in you, Mr Garwood—a large bit!'

Sara's mouth tightened as she held on to her reserved composure. The 'artist in residence' crack had apparently been made to explain her less than housekeeperish attire. However, from the expressions on the faces of the crew, it was obvious that the word 'artist' had conjured up the Bohemian stereotype, leaving no doubt in their minds that her true position was that of Brad Garwood's mistress.

And, as it turned out, the smartly dressed, uniformed cleaning service people were only the beginning. While they were still in the house, a policeman came to ask Brad more questions concerning the accident. This time he introduced Sara only as his housekeeper. The policeman took one look at her trim figure housed in faded denims and a tee-shirt and his eyes told Sara that he didn't believe the housekeeper story either.

Retreating to her studio, she tried to push the sidelong glances out of her mind, with only limited success. Each time she was forced out of her seclusion to change Brad's ice packs, she encountered at least one member of the crew, and then there was the policeman watching her every move. By eleven-thirty when the house crew had finished and Kate sought her out for an inspection tour of the work done, her nerves were taut as a bowstring. Briefly, Sara allowed herself to believe that Kate had sought her out for a complete inspection because after seeing that she had her own bedroom, the woman had decided to believe that she actually was the housekeeper. However, as they moved from room to room, Kate's less than subtle probing let Sara know that she was only after more details of the arrangement.

Feigning ignorance, Sara made only comments pertaining to the work the crew had done and managed to get them out of the house before totally losing her temper.

Hearing Brad bringing the policeman down to show him out, she ducked into the kitchen. One more knowing look from a stranger and she wasn't certain if she could control herself!

'You're muttering to yourself again,' Brad commented drily, entering the kitchen as she was finishing preparing his sandwich.

'It's this double standard society we live in,' she hissed. 'For a man to have a mistress, it's a boost to his reputation; for a woman to be one, it's a black mark on her name.'

'Are we talking about anyone in particular?' he questioned innocently.

'You know perfectly well what I'm talking about,' she glared. 'Kate and her crew, and even the policeman, are all certain that I'm your mistress.'

'Yes, I did get that impression,' he admitted, much in the manner of an adult who was witnessing a child learning one of life's lesson the hard way. 'Maybe it was the jeans. They do fit a bit snugly. And that tee-shirt . . . I never realised a tee-shirt could be so . . . definitive.'

'You may find this amusing,' she snapped, losing her temper completely, 'but I find it very difficult being seen as a scarlet woman!'

'I suppose there's the possibility that I'll have to marry you to save you from the gossipmongers,' Brad mused, leaning against the counter, obviously enjoying her discomfort.

'Don't be ridiculous!' Her chin came up defiantly as she used her anger to hide the sharp jab of pain his mockingly delivered solution had produced. 'Besides, people expect artists to have lovers. You certainly jumped to that conclusion.'

'I thought your reputation was important to you,' he challenged, straightening away from the counter, his one good hand hooked into his pants pocket as he stood towering over her.

'I'm sure I can live down one off-colour episode,' Sara faced him haughtily.

'First you find me ridiculous and now I'm an off-colour episode,' he glowered, green fire flashing in his eyes. 'There are moments, woman . . .'

As he spoke, he crossed the distance between them. Suddenly a steel band circled Sara and she found herself pulled hard against his solid form.

Her lips were parted in the beginning of a protest when his mouth found hers, giving the contact an immediate sense of intimacy. Her senses reeled as liquid fire surged through her veins, then sanity was lost in a whirlwind of emotion.

She was so very intensely aware of the feel of him. Even his injured hand, which rested lightly on her hip, seemed to burn its imprint into her.

Responding to the increasingly sensual demand of his kiss, she strained against his virile male frame, her hands caressing the expanse of his chest before moving over his shoulders.

Brad flinched as she found a spot left tender by the accident, and the sharp memory of his earlier rejection impinged harshly into her world of mindless sensations. As a semblance of sanity fought its way to the surface, she began to struggle.

Almost immediately she pushed against another still tender bruise. Unable to bring herself to consciously hurt him, she dropped her hands to her sides and stood rigid in his embrace.

'Damn!' he muttered under his breath, drawing away from her and releasing her so suddenly, she had to catch the table to steady herself.

Her lips tightened into a hard straight line to keep her chin from trembling as she watched him stride out of the room without a backward glance. 'The male ego is certainly a fragile thing,' she muttered bitterly, while attempting to erase the taste of his mouth from her lips with the back of her hand. It didn't work. The feel of him, from the taut hard thigh muscles pressed against her softer contours to the hot demanding pressure of his mouth, lingered.

'He really would have been shocked if I'd accepted his

joking suggestion of marriage as a solution,' she continued her one-sided conversation, curving her mouth into what was supposed to be a cynical smile but which missed the mark and instead gave her a wistfully forlorn appearance as angry tears filled her eyes. Blinking them back, she refused to let her irrational response to the man dominate her reason.

Carrying his sandwich along with a drink into the dining room, she found Brad standing, staring out the window, his back turned towards her. He did not acknowledge her presence and she did not speak to him. Staying only long enough to place the food on the table, she made a hasty retreat.

Back in the kitchen, she tried to eat, but her sandwich caught in her throat and she tossed it into the waste bin after only a couple of bites.

Later, climbing the stairs to her studio, she chided herself for letting the man unhinge her. What he did or thought was of no consequence to her. 'It shouldn't be, anyway,' she muttered, uncovering the clay head and staring at the rough countenance.

In an uncontrolled movement, her fingers traced the line of the jaw. Her touch resembled more of a caress than an artistic moulding, and once again her mother's words returned to haunt her. 'I can't possibly be in love with the man. He's difficult and arrogant,' she mumbled, then was forced to amend this harsh judgment as she recalled Brad's easy manner with the children and the instances when he had admitted to being less than perfect. Still, she had only known him for a few days. In spite of her recent erratic behaviour she was normally a quiet, rational, thoughtful person. She firmly believed that before two people could be truly in love they had to spend time together; see if their interests were compatible; find out if their temperaments were complementary. A person didn't fall in love with a man just because he had green eyes that could flash fire or soothed like velvet or because his touch evoked certain erotic responses.

She was still denying any emotional involvement when the doorbell rang in the middle of the afternoon. Forgetting to remove her smock, she opened the door in a slightly breathless condition from her run down three flights of stairs to find herself face to face with Marc and Monica Fallon.

Marc was the first to recover. 'We heard about the accident and came over to see how Brad's getting along,' he said, his eyes bright with amusement.

'But if he's busy, we don't want to disturb him.' Monica's expression was schooled into one of stiff politeness.

'Please come in,' Sara requested, forcing an indifference into her voice and a formal smile on her face as she self-consciously smoothed the paint-smeared smock she wore.

'I really don't think we can stay,' Monica balked.

'Of course we can,' said Marc, taking his sister's arm and guiding her up the stairs behind Sara, who found the gleam in the man's eyes disconcerting. Although Monica Fallon was throwing her periodic glances, she felt pretty certain that the woman had not recognised her. Marc, on the other hand, had obviously placed her immediately.

'Who may I say is calling?' she asked after ushering them into the living room on the second floor.

'Monica and Marc Fallon,' Marc responded pleasantly, apparently willing to play the game; at least, for now.

Excusing herself to announce their presence, Sara paused outside the partly closed door for a moment to stop the shaking which had suddenly come over her. From inside she heard Monica ask her brother in a refined, hushed whisper, 'Who do you think she is?'

'Probably a house painter,' he replied, his voice at a natural level as he made no effort to match his sister's discreet behaviour. 'With Women's Lib, one never knows where a female will turn up next or what role she'll be playing.'

Running a hand through her hair, Sara turned towards the stairs, only to almost collide with Brad. 'The Fallons are in the living room,' she managed in calm tones.

'So I heard,' he frowned. 'Please prepare some coffee for Marc and myself. Monica will take tea.'

'Yes, sir.' Sara was past him and down the steps before he entered the room where his guests waited. After turning the water on to boil and starting a fresh pot of coffee, she went into her room to run a brush through her hair. Seeing herself in the mirror, dressed in her jeans, tee-shirt, and Steve's oversized, paint-smeared shirt acting as a smock, she cringed. Compared to Monica Fallon, who sat poised gracefully on the antique Victorian sofa upstairs in her tailored Paris suit with its slit skirt and lace blouse, Sara felt like a beggar's daughter. She considered changing, but stopped herself. 'I'm not in competition with Monica Fallon,' she stated emphatically to the dubious image in the mirror. She did, however, exchange the smock for a pinafore-style apron which covered her tee-shirt and half of her jeans before carrying the refreshments upstairs.

'I know it's none of my business, because once you own the property, you have the right to do with it what you wish,' Monica was saying as Sara walked into the living room. 'But I'm curious to know what you plan for Cyprus Point. Are you going to tear down the house and build another of your "communities"?' In spite of the woman's attempt to hide her feelings, there was a hint of sadness in her voice as she spoke of this prospect.

'You have every right to ask,' Brad assured her. 'Cyprus Point has been in your family for centuries. The answer is no, I do not plan to tear down the house nor to cut up the remaining land. The architectural design of the building is far too valuable to be destroyed, not to mention the history surrounding the place. I plan to renovate it, keeping as much of the original structure as possible, and then move into it as my personal residence.'

'I'm so glad!' Monica smiled up at him, relief written on her features. 'It's a wonderful place to raise a family. I recall my childhood there with intense delight.'

Brad returned Monica's smile and Sara's knuckles whitened on the handles of the tray she was carrying.

'Everyone to their own poison,' Marc muttered. Then in stronger tones, almost in the same style as that of a ham actor who has decided that it is time for him to take centre stage, he said, 'Actually, Father was furious when he heard about the accident. He's afraid old Hanna's curse is going to prevent him from ever selling the place.'

'Marc, really!' Monica flushed.

'I didn't know there was actually a curse,' said Brad, showing interest but no concern.

'Oh, yes. Father swore us to secrecy, but since there've been two deaths already and now you've had a very close call, I suppose there's no harm in telling,' Marc mused. It was obvious from his manner and voice that he was enjoying this little game.

'Marc, I really don't think Brad is interested in a dying woman's ravings,' Monica attempted to stop him.

'Of course he is,' Marc assured her with an indulgent brotherly air. 'He's buying or, at least, trying to buy Hanna's sacred little kingdom.'

Setting the laden tray down on the coffee table, Sara glanced up in time to catch the warning in the man's eyes as he looked towards Brad, and a spasm of fear shook her.

'Actually we should have recorded it on film,' he continued, a hint of sarcasm entering his voice. 'It could have been the opening of one of those horrible gothic murder mysteries. There was old Hanna on her deathbed with the family dutifully though grudgingly gathered around. I remember her eyes were closed and I thought she was already dead, when suddenly they opened and there was that fierceness in them that had always cowed me as a child. She stared straight at my father. "I know you're going to try to get rid of Cyprus Point the moment I'm dead,' she said, 'but I warn you. No one but a person of Halloway ancestry will ever live here. It was Halloway sweat that cleared this land and Halloway blood that was shed in two wars to keep it. When my family lost their fortune and were forced to sell this home, I forsook the man I loved and married your father instead to ensure that Halloway blood would always flow through the veins of those who dwelt here. You will not thwart me. I cannot bring myself to place a curse on anyone of my own flesh, but I do curse any outsider who would attempt to make Cyprus Point his home".' Marc's voice had become a high-pitched whine containing a vindictive threatening quality as he mimicked the elderly woman's manner.

The sensation of dread Sara had been experiencing off and on lately returned with renewed force.

'Marc, you're embarrassing me!' Monica raised a delicate, well-manicured hand to her cheek as if to test the warmth of her skin. 'No one believes in curses and superstitions today.'

'I'd suggest that Brad might consider the possibility,' Marc persisted undaunted, his eyes travelling from the wrapped wrist to the bandaged face.

'Tea, Miss Fallon?' Sara broke the stilted silence following this observation as she fought to regain some semblance of normality within herself and the atmosphere in general. Monica was right. Curses and superstitions belonged in a different time and age. Still . . .

'Yes, please,' the dark-haired woman replied, forcing a smile. She was obviously having a difficult time hiding her anger towards her brother.

'Of course, you could possibly ward off the curse by marrying Monica right away,' Marc suggested with a mischievous gleam in his eyes. 'Though considering dear old Hanna's aversion to Yankees, she might consider my sister better off a widow once the property was in her hands.'

'I don't enjoy your less than flattering insinuation that Brad would marry me simply to ward off a curse,' Monica frowned.

'You're much too beautiful to be associated with any curse,' Brad assured her gallantly.

'And for a Yankee, you can be most charming,' she purred in return.

'Coffee or tea, Mr Fallon?' asked Sara, controlling the tremor that threatened to invade her voice. Again she told herself that she didn't care what Brad Garwood did or said, but this time the lie crumbled immediately. She felt as green as his eyes.

'I'd prefer something a bit stiffer. It's after twelve.' Though the request was made to Brad, Marc's attention focused on Sara.

Walking over to the walnut liquor cabinet built into the wall, Brad opened the intricately carved door. 'Bourbon?' he questioned over his shoulder.

'Straight,' Marc stipulated, continuing to concentrate on Sara.

'Coffee, Mr Garwood?' she questioned, feeling decidedly uneasy and wanting only to finish serving and escape.

'Yes, please,' he replied, handing Marc his drink before turning to accept his cup from her.

All three were standing very close and the heat of Marc's gaze was causing Sara's hands to sweat. 'I don't believe you've introduced this most charming addition to your household,' Marc addressed Brad. 'Don't tell me that blue jeans are the newest uniform for nurses.'

'Sara is my temporary housekeeper,' Brad replied, his tone indifferent as if he found her presence a necessary bore.

'If she's looking for a more permanent position, I'm suddenly very seriously considering finding a place of my own.' Marc's voice held only the slightest hint of suggestiveness as he raised his glass in salute.

'Sara is not a housekeeper by profession,' Brad explained. 'She's an artist, and when she lost her apartment I offered her a position in my home until she could find other suitable quarters. Her family are well known to me and I felt compelled to aid her.'

Inwardly, Sara bristled, while outwardly she maintained an air of reserved calm. She knew that Brad was merely attempting to assure Monica that he had no designs on his housekeeper, but he didn't have to make the situation sound so totally disagreeable where he was concerned. Then, in a more reasonable turn of mind, she realised that he was also protecting her reputation and that she should be grateful. However, gratitude and jealousy did not mix well.

'How very gallant of you,' Marc smiled drily. 'I suppose fledgling artists do find it difficult to live on their work alone.'

'You do look familiar,' Monica broke into the conversation, as she concentrated her attention on Sara too. 'Perhaps I've seen you at an exhibition.'

'Perhaps,' Sara managed in a calm tone. 'Though I do have a very average appearance and am always being told I remind people of someone else.'

'I suppose that could be the case,' Monica mused in her soft Southern drawl, her hand going to smooth her black tresses as if to say she had never had the misfortune of being nondescript.

'Do you have a gallery?' Marc enquired, a touch of indulgent amusement towards his sister curling one corner of his mouth slightly.

'Some of my works are on display at the Grimes Gallery,' Sara replied, backing towards the door. 'Now, if you'll excuse me, I do have dinner to prepare.'

Brad nodded his dismissal and she was gone before either of the Fallons could ask any more questions. Her escape, however, was not successful.

'I've decided I want some ice to chill this Bourbon,' Marc announced suddenly, his voice carrying to her out on the landing. 'So I'll just accompany your housekeeper to the kitchen. That will save her a trip back upstairs.' Before anyone could offer an objection, he was out the door and by Sara's side.

'I must apologise for Marc,' Monica's embarrassed tones floated out of the living room. 'I don't know what's got into him lately.'

'Maybe it's the alcohol,' Marc suggested mischievously into Sara's ear as they continued down the stairs. 'Or maybe I'm beginning to believe in fairy tales. The prince did, after all, rediscover Cinderella and she was acting as the scullerymaid. The coincidence is too much to be dismissed as anything less than fate.'

Inwardly Sara cringed at this overt admission of recognition and quickened her step, not wanting to take a chance that Marc might raise his voice and give her away to his sister. 'I thought you'd cast yourself in the role of my Fairy Godfather,' she reminded him as they went into the kitchen and she took his glass.

'I've decided to recast myself. You're much too lovely and interesting a heroine for me not to want to play the hero.' Suddenly a pained look flashed across his face. 'Or do you already have your Prince Charming?' he questioned, indicating the second floor with an upward glance.

'No, I do not have a Prince Charming,' she frowned indulgently as she handed him his drink now diluted with ice.

'Only a lecherous Yankee?' The words came out more as a question than a jest.

'He's not lecherous. He's my employer and behaves in the utmost proper manner towards me,' Sara stated firmly.

'Then I can assume you have separate sleeping quarters,' he queried bluntly as he downed the drink in one smooth swallow. Sara guessed it was not his first of the day.

'My room is on this floor. Mr Garwood sleeps on the third floor,' she responded frostily, her patience wearing thin.

'I love it!' Marc smiled broadly. 'This is becoming more and more like the original story with every moment . . . our heroine lives near the kitchen! I insist on playing Prince Charming!'

'Then why don't you return to your sister and Mr Garwood before you get me into trouble?' she suggested tightly.

'Only after you tell me the real story of why you're

here.' His expression was adamant and she knew she would have to tell him something.

'Mr Garwood recognised me at the party,' she began hesitantly.

'You keep calling him Mr Garwood,' Marc interrupted. 'According to his version, he's an old family friend.'

'He's a friend of my family's, not a friend of mine.' The coolness in her voice verged on splintered ice.

'So you would have the world believe.' He raised a sceptical eyebrow and then lowered it. 'However, the prince never questioned Cinderella's integrity and I won't blotch the story line now by questioning yours. Now tell me, how exactly did you get from the party to this job?'

'As I said,' Sara began again, allowing indignant anger to flash in her eyes, 'he recognised me at the party. When I left, he followed me and demanded to know what I was up to. I explained about my freelance writing to support myself while I pursued a career in art and he offered me a bargain. If I wouldn't send in any stories about your sister and her friends, he would provide me with a job in which I could earn a living wage and still have plenty of time to devote to my art.'

'And the noble Mr Garwood has made no advances towards his lovely scullerymaid?' Before the words were totally out, Marc's hand went up in a gesture of self-defence. 'I wasn't questioning your integrity, Sara, only that of your employer.'

'He sees himself in the role of my reluctant guardian,' she said, attempting to remain civil but finding it more and more difficult as her nerves continued to fray.

'Men have a way of changing roles,' he reminded her pointedly.

'Monica is ready to leave,' Brad's cold tones sounded from the doorway before Sara could respond.

'I'll be there in a minute,' Marc threw over his shoulder with indifferent calm. Then taking Sara's hand he carried it to his lips. 'I don't believe you told me your last name.'

'It's Manderly,' she flushed, poignantly aware of Brad's icy stare as he remained in the doorway waiting for his capricious guest.

'We shall meet again, Sara Manderly, and next time I'll remember to bring the glass slipper,' Marc promised.

'Goodbye, Mr Fallon,' she frowned selfconsciously, slipping her hand free and moving towards the refrigerator.

Although this ploy allowed her to turn her back towards the two men as Marc joined his host, she still felt Brad's eyes on her as if it was a physical contact. Relief came only as the door swung closed.

It was, however, a shortlived relief. 'What was all that about a glass slipper?' Brad demanded, re-entering the kitchen only minutes later.

'It's a long story and I prefer not to go into it,' she snapped back, still picturing him smiling down on Monica Fallon.

'I don't care what you prefer,' he returned icily. 'What Marc Fallon knows about you could be dangerous to me. Since he now knows your surname, he could very easily discover that your brother works for me as my Chief of Security. Putting two and two together and coming up with five, he could decide that you're here to ensure my safety.'

'You mean like one of those female karate experts who can take out ten men with a couple of kicks and punches,' she questioned sarcastically, 'or am I allowed to be the "Charlie's Angel" type? If I get a choice, I prefer the gun-toting, classy lady image who uses her brains rather than her other body parts.'

Angrily, Brad caught her by the shoulders. 'Sara, this is no joking matter. Rumours of trouble can be very damaging and take a long time to die.' Then suddenly, as if realising for the first time that he was touching her, he released her abruptly.

'Marc doesn't think I'm here protecting you,' she said, her chin coming up defiantly. 'I repeated the business about you being an old family friend. Then I told him that you'd recognised me at the party and when you found out that I was planning to write stories about Monica and her friends to support myself until my career in art was established, you offered me this job on condition that I submitted no such stories. So you see, I painted you as his "charmin' sister's" anonymous hero.'

'And he bought it?'

'I'm sure he did. He seems to be under the impression that you're planning to marry the woman. It would only be natural for you to want to protect her from villainous, opportunistic females like myself.' This came out with a strong touch of acid, and Sara mentally berated herself for allowing her emotions to show.

'Let's just hope you're right!' he growled.

'Sara's nearly always right,' Steve's voice came through the back door screen. 'But what's she right about this time?'

'Marc Fallon,' she replied, unlatching the door and letting her brother inside, relieved to have a third party present. Jealousy was not an emotion she was experienced in handling and it was beginning to glow like a neon light through her remarks. 'He and his sister were just here and our mutual employer is afraid that Marc will discover that I'm your sister and leap to the conclusion that I'm actually here as a bodyguard rather than a housekeeper. But I'm certain that thought will never enter his mind.'

'Wrapped him around your little finger, Sis?' Steve quipped, grinning widely.

'No, I didn't,' she retorted.

Sensing that he had made a tactical error, Steve dropped the subject of Marc Fallon, at least for the moment. 'Got any coffee?'

'Of course,' she answered, modifying her tone, embarrassed that she had reacted so strongly to her brother's playful bantering.

'Did you come by to see me or to check on your sister?' Brad questioned, a hint of anger still present in his voice. 'Because if you came to visit with Sara, I'll leave the two of you alone. I still have work to do.'

'Actually, it's a little of both,' Steve replied, accepting the requested cup of coffee from Sara and seating himself at the kitchen table. 'I wanted to see how you were doing and I always like to check in on my sister from time to time.'

Catching the protective undertone in her brother's voice, Sara threw him an exasperated glance.

'As you can see, I'm doing just fine.' There was an indefinable quality in Brad's voice which caused Sara to glance towards him, but his expression was shuttered.

'I spent some time out at The Pines this afternoon,' Steve continued, his manner becoming strictly businesslike.

Sara pulled a chicken out of the refrigerator and began cutting it up as the men talked.

'And what did you find?' Brad asked, pouring himself a cup of coffee and leaning against the counter while he drank it.

'Nothing really. A little before you received your call, a woman had reported some activity in the woods near the construction entrance. Two of our men went out to check, but they didn't find anything. Ray was already out making his regular rounds, but that still left Chuck by the phone. Either the woman who called you never tried to call the local security people or she got so flustered she dialled the wrong number and when it was busy called you.'

'But there was no damage done?' Brad questioned sharply.

'No, none that we could find, and nothing was stolen. It was probably that same group of kids that ran the caterpillar into the lake. When they saw all the security people running around the place, it must have scared them off. I doubt if they'll be back.'

'Good. But keep the extra men there for another week or so,' Brad directed, setting down his coffee cup and preparing to leave.

'There is one little thing that's been bothering me,' said Steve, delaying the man's departure. Sara knew her brother well and her ears perked up as she caught the subtle undertone in his voice. 'The woman who called you . . . are you sure she didn't say who she was or what unit she lived in?'

'She was pretty hysterical,' Brad replied, shaking his head in a negative gesture. 'She could barely get out the information that she was at The Pines. Why?'

'I did some door-to-door canvassing this afternoon,' Steve frowned. 'And I couldn't find a single tenant who was willing to admit to having made either phone call.'

'Were you able to question all of them?' Brad questioned.

'No, not everyone was at home,' Steve admitted, adding, 'And it could have been one of them who called or it could be that the person who called didn't want to admit the fact. They could be afraid that the vandals might find out who reported them and harass them. It's just that I don't like loose ends.'

'As long as no harm was done, I'm satisfied,' Brad said tersely, obviously anxious to return to his work. 'Now, if you'll excuse me, I'll leave you to visit with your sister.'

'I wouldn't exactly say no harm was done,' Sara muttered as the door swung closed following his departure.

'No, not exactly,' Steve agreed quietly. Then coming to stand by his sister, he said, 'I think it's time for you to tell me what was going on when I arrived.'

'The Fallons came,' she replied sharply.

'That part I know. What I don't know is what happened while they were here that set both you and Brad on edge. Did they recognise you?'

'Monica didn't. Marc did, but he didn't give me away to his sister. Brad told them both that he was friendly with my family and had given me this job as a temporary measure when I lost my apartment. Anyway, later, Marc followed me down to the kitchen and demanded to know the truth. I told him that Brad was a friend of my family just like he'd said and that he'd recognised me at the party and had given me this job in exchange for my word that I wouldn't write any stories about Monica and her friends. Remember, the reason he took me into the ball was that he thought I was writing for one of those yellow tabloids.'

'And he bought it?'

'He wasn't totally convinced that Brad wasn't attempting to take advantage of me while I was under his roof, but he bought the rest of the story. He thinks Brad wants to marry his sister, so it would only follow that he would do what he could to protect her.'

Although Sara tried to keep her manner and tone indifferent, Steve knew her too well not to recognise that something was bothering her. 'If you're worried about what Marc Fallon thinks of you, don't be,' he said. 'The man is a useless lush.'

'What Marc thinks of me doesn't matter,' she frowned.

'Then what's causing that dark cloud hanging over your head?' he persisted.

'It's not a dark cloud. It's just some confusion,' she replied defensively. 'I simply don't understand what a man like Brad Garwood, who's worked hard all his life, can see in a woman whose whole life is spent worrying about what dress she's going to wear to her next party or who'll sit next to whom at dinner.'

'I think you're being a little rough on Monica Fallon,' Steve cautioned. 'I understand she does a great deal of charity work. As far as the attraction between men and women is concerned, it's not based on reason. It's just something that happens.'

'Apparently,' she muttered, pushing the chicken into the oven and washing her hands. Then, beginning to feel uncomfortable under Steve's continued scrutiny, she decided to change the direction of the conversation before she admitted more than she wanted to. 'There was something else that happened during the Fallons' visit that disturbed me,' she began, then hesitated, suddenly feeling very guilty about telling Steve any details of Brad's private life. It made it look as if she was in his house to provide her brother with information.

'And what was that?' he coaxed, as her hesitation lengthened into a prolonged silence. 'You have good instincts, Sis. If something has upset you, you should tell me.'

'It's probably nothing,' she hedged. Then because it really was bothering her and because she knew Steve would not give up until she told him, she said slowly, 'Marc went into a detailed account of how his grandmother had placed a deathbed curse on anyone who was not a Halloway or married to a Halloway who attempted to live at Cyprus Point. He seemed determined to create the impression that Brad could be in danger.'

'Then there actually is a curse,' Steve mused.

'Apparently so. It seems that their father had sworn them to secrecy because he was afraid he might not be able to sell the place.'

'You know I don't believe in curses and superstitions, but I have to admit that two prior deaths does make me a bit uneasy,' said Steve, deep furrows creasing his brow as he added, 'I wonder why Fallon brought up the curse.'

'I had the distinct impression that he was trying to warn Brad. He was not particularly subtle in his insinuation that the accident could have had something to do with the purchase of Cyprus Point. He even suggested that if Brad wanted to remain safe he should marry Monica.' Sara's mouth tightened at the remembered suggestion.

'What did Monica have to say about all this?' Steve questioned.

'She was embarrassed by her brother's remarks. I guess she's afraid people will think he's a bit eccentric.'

'What he is, is an alcoholic,' Steve stated with disgust. 'You would think that someone with his opportunities in life would have made something better of himself.'

'True,' Sara admitted. 'Now, so that I don't feel like a spy, could we change the subject? Why did you come by to see me? Surely you aren't checking up on me?'

'The weekly letter from Mom came today.' A playfully remorseful expression appeared on his face as he handed her the two neatly written pages.

Reading through it quickly. Sara paled as she reached the last paragraph. 'She's coming home two weeks from yesterday?' she muttered.

'You're going to have to do some fast apartment hunting,' he nodded.

'I'd planned to be out of here by the end of next week, anyway, I had just hoped to have a little more time for Joanie and Tommy to have forgotten about Brad Garwood,' she sighed. 'You know what chatterboxes they are.'

'Just so you're out of here before it's more than Tommy and Joanie who are doing the talking,' Steve warned.

Sara merely grimaced, not having the nerve to tell him about the policeman and the cleaning service people.

Following Steve's departure, she went up to the living room to collect the coffee and tea things left from the afternoon visitors. As she replaced the cup used by Monica on the tray, she wished she hadn't mentioned the business about the curse to Steve. It made her feel like a child carrying tales. But then there had been a flavour to Marc's remarks that had left her feeling edgy.

Frowning introspectively, she sat down in one of the graceful Victorian chairs near the fireplace and stared with unseeing eyes at the empty hearth. It wasn't Marc who had made her edgy. It was Monica. Monica and Brad. She remembered what a handsome couple they made, in their nineteenth-century costumes, floating across the floor to the strains of a waltz. Grudgingly she admitted that Monica would be the perfect wife for a successful businessman. She knew all the right people and how to entertain them. In addition to which, there was the prestige of the Fallon name.

Slowly a tear trickled down her cheek. How could she care so deeply for a man who had come into her life only days earlier and who treated her as if she were a child who needed constant guidance?

'For Pete's sake, what's wrong?' Brad's voice sliced

through the air as he strode across the room and knelt in front of her. 'Did Steve bring some bad news?'

'No,' she managed to choke out as she brushed away the tear with a quick, nervous gesture. 'I had something in my eye, but it's gone.'

His hand came up to touch the still damp flesh, then immediately breaking the contact, he straightened and moved away to stand leaning against the mantel above the fireplace.

'I'm sorry if my presence embarrassed you today,' she said stiffly. 'I hope Monica wasn't upset.'

'Monica is a very generous and understanding woman,' he replied, hooking his thumbs in his pockets as he faced her. 'And I told no lies. I consider Steve a friend as well as a valued employee, and you did lose your apartment and needed a place to stay until you were resettled.'

Sara thought that she would not have been so understanding if the roles had been reversed, but she said nothing. The truth could be that Monica was simply better at hiding her emotions than most women.

Brad continued to watch her. It was obvious he had not believed the 'something in the eye' story. 'Did Steve come by for some special reason, or does he always check up on you once a day?'

'He brought over the weekly letter from our mother. She's coming home in a few days. But you don't have to worry, I'll be out of here by then,' she replied tightly, wondering if Brad was again going to accuse her of working for her brother and suggest that Steve's appearance was more of a business call than a brother-sister visit. Then realising that it was her own conscience that was bothering her, she said, 'I did mention the story Marc told about his grandmother placing a curse on Cyprus Point to Steve.'

'You did?' A sardonic smile curled his lips as if she was verifying his suspicion that she was her brother's spy.

'Yes, I did,' she glared up at him defensively. 'He seemed to be warning you.'

'Did it ever occur to you that he was merely putting on a show for your benefit?' Brad questioned drily.

'A show for my benefit?!' Her eyes widened as she stared at the man incredulously.

'I noticed he found it impossible to stay away from you. Perhaps he wanted to be certain you understood how extensive his bloodlines are.'

'I'm not a social climber, Mr Garwood. The Fallon and Halloway names hold no importance for me.' She faced him haughtily, her mouth tightening into a hard line as she bit back the words which threatened to follow as an image of Monica flashed through her mind. Rising abruptly from the chair, she retrieved the tray and strode from the room.

During dinner, she singlemindedly perused the classified adds, circling even those that looked only halfway promising.

'Find anything?' Brad broke into her concentration as he entered the kitchen.

'Several possibilities,' she replied, then demanded as he started pouring himself a cup of coffee, 'Why didn't you ring?'

'I didn't see any reason to get used to being waited on hand and foot when I'll be losing my housekeeper one day soon.'

There was an underlying hint of anticipation in his voice that rankled. 'I'm certain you'll find someone who can do a much better job than I've done,' she returned frostily.

'Actually,' he said, pausing at the door to give her his

full attention, 'I'm considering a more permanent type of arrangement, which is another reason for not allowing myself to get too used to being waited on. I understand the modern female doesn't believe in subservience to her spouse.'

Acid rose in Sara's throat. So he was planning to ask Monica to marry him. Well, if he thought Monica Fallon was going to live without both a cook and a maid to wait on her hand and foot, he was in for a shock, Sara thought sarcastically. Not trusting the pain to be totally removed from her eyes, she picked up her newspaper and, feigning intense interest in the printed page, said in an indifferent tone, 'Then it's a good thing I'm moving out very soon. I wouldn't want to complicate your plans by my presence.'

The hairs on the back of her neck prickled as she felt his eyes on her for a long moment, then abruptly he left.

As the door swung closed behind him, her shoulders sagged and she squeezed her eyes shut in an attempt to block out the image of him and Monica together. 'I wonder how old Hanna will feel about having little half-Yankees running around her plantation,' she muttered hostilely, brushing away an offensive tear that had somehow escaped.

Clearing away the dishes, she told herself for the thousandth time that she was being ridiculous to allow herself to react so strongly to a man she had known for only days. The problem was that she didn't feel as if she had known him for only a few days. She felt as if she had always known him. It was as if he was the missing piece of her world which she had been searching for all this time; a necessary integral to make her existence complete.

'A person would think you were a schoolgirl, the way you're overreacting to the man,' she scolded herself as she finished the last pan and dried her hands.

Tossing the newspaper on to her bed, she went up to her studio, intent on finishing the bust and putting Brad Garwood behind her for ever. Once she was gone from his house, she was determined that he would be gone from her life.

However, as she worked and reworked the clay, the task began to feel impossible. The problem was the ears; no matter what she did they still didn't look right. Finally she admitted defeat and knocked on Brad's workroom door.

'What is it?' he asked, glancing up impatiently from his draught board.

'Nothing. Excuse me for interrupting,' she flushed, suddenly willing to give up totally on the sculpture rather than spend any length of time studying the man's features in the flesh. Closing the door, she walked rapidly back into her studio and began wrapping the clay. Tomorrow was Saturday, and she would find a new place to live and be rid of Brad Garwood.

A knock on the studio door followed by Brad's entrance brought her to a stop in mid-motion. 'Do you need me to sit again?' he asked, his manner controlled and she guessed that he was tiring of her presence rapidly.

'I didn't mean to interrupt,' she apologised tightly.

'I needed to take a break anyway. Shall I use the same stool as before?'

Sara had a tremendous urge to tell him to go away. But realising how foolish that would make her look since she had been the one to seek him out in the first place, she said, 'Yes, that will be fine.'

As she began to work, she discovered to her dismay that even her art was no protection against the force of Brad's presence. With him so near, she could not concentrate and the ears still refused to look correct. As a last resort, in an effort to understand the shape, she walked over to him and ran her fingers along the contours of the lobe.

His jaw went rigid as he stiffened away from her touch. Then as if he felt he needed to offer some sort of explanation, he said briskly, 'Your hand is cold.'

'I'm sorry.' Her words came out with a caustic quality as she fought back the pain. 'I seem to be unable to get the shape right. I think I'll stop for tonight.'

'Fine,' he muttered, rising and leaving immediately.

Her hands shook as she recovered the clay. How could she be in love with a man who found her so unappealing that he cringed at her touch?

# CHAPTER SIX

AFTER a restless night, Sara awoke the next morning to the smell of bacon frying and coffee perking. Dressing hurriedly, she went into the kitchen to find Brad breaking eggs into the skillet. The table was set for two.

'It's about time you were getting up,' he said over his shoulder.

'You should have woken me,' she yawned, noticing how the muscles of his back moved beneath the fabric of his shirt. Then, angry with herself, she diverted her attention to the clock on the wall. It read six-thirty. She had overslept, but not by much, considering the fact that this was Saturday. 'I would have made your breakfast. You're still supposed to use your wrist as little as possible.'

'My wrist feels much better,' he professed, although she noticed that he was doing nearly everything one-handed. 'Besides, it's Saturday and this is your weekend off.' As he dished up the eggs on to the plates, he added, 'I made enough for two. Will you join me?'

Hesitantly, Sara sat down at the table. The back door was open, letting in the soft scent of lilac from the garden.

'I'm not a bad cook,' Brad assured her. Even the hint of amusement in his eyes could not mask the traces of tiredness. Obviously he was not sleeping well and she guessed his wrist was bothering him more than he wanted to admit.

'It looks delicious,' she murmured, confused by his attentiveness. It was a confusion that did not last long.

'I've been thinking,' he said between bites. 'I'll be closing the deal on Cyprus Point this week. As soon as the papers are signed I plan to move out there to personally direct the renovations, and that will leave this house unoccupied. It's occurred to me that you could stay on here as a sort of caretaker. I don't want you rushing into a lease on an apartment that would be unsuitable. Besides, someone should be here to look after the place.

'It's really unnecessary for you to move out of your home to be rid of me. I'm sure I'll find a suitable residence this weekend and be gone by the middle of the week.' Sara rose awkwardly, anger holding back her tears as she headed towards her room.

'Damn it, Sara!' Brad caught her by the shoulders before she could make good her escape. Keeping her back towards him, his hands closed around her upper arms, holding her captive. 'You've got this all wrong.'

'I apologise for overreacting,' she said, forcing herself to sound reasonably calm. 'I realise that you only want to clear the way for your wife.'

'Your being in this house with me at Cyprus Point won't interfere . . .'

'That's impossible,' she interrupted hotly. 'People will say I'm your in-town mistress, and I'm sure even your very understanding Monica Fallon wouldn't agree to such a situation!' Twisting out of his grasp, she grabbed the newspaper and her handbag from her room and stormed back through the kitchen.

'Sara!' Brad said her name in an exasperated tone as if he was trying to reason with a child.

Ignoring him, she slammed out the back door and climbed into her car. She didn't know which she hated worse, his big brother routine or the times when he acted as if he couldn't stand to have her around. She only knew that he had her on an emotional rollercoaster and she intended to get off as soon as possible.

By noon she was feeling thoroughly depressed. The only reasonable place she had found would not be available until the middle of the next month. Stopping by the house for a sandwich, she found a note from Brad saying that he had gone to pick up his car and that Margarete Grimes had called and wanted Sara to call her back.

Pouring herself a glass of orange juice, Sara dialled the number for the gallery.

Margarete was absolutely bubbling when she came to the phone. 'You must have made quite a conquest,' she teased laughingly.

'Conquest?' Sara questioned, hot and tired and in no mood for games.

'Marc Fallon was waiting outside when I opened up this morning,' Margarete elaborated.

'Marc?' Sara muttered.

'Yes, Marc. Why didn't you tell me you knew the Fallons?'

'I don't really know them well,' Sara defended, developing a very uneasy feeling in the pit of her stomach.

'Well, you must have impressed Marc. He bought every piece of your work I had,' Margarete laughed.

'Every one?' Sara choked.

'Every one. Even the ones you had asked me to store, both the paintings and the sculptures.'

'Every one?' Sara repeated, too stunned to think.

'Every one,' Margarete reaffirmed. 'He muttered something about a "glass slipper", but I've heard he's a bit eccentric. Anyway, that doesn't matter. Having a Fallon, even an eccentric, for a sponsor practically ensures your success as a recognised artist in Charleston.'

'Glass slipper?' Sara frowned, her shock turning swiftly to anger.

'Yes, dear. Now it's imperative that you bring me more. Once he hangs his, I expect other customers will be coming in soon looking for your work.'

'I'll get back to you,' Sara managed, almost too furious to speak. Hanging up the phone before Margarete could protest, she stormed out of the house.

By the time she reached the Fallon home, her anger had reached the stage of a red fury, causing the staid butler to look dubiously into her flushed face when she requested to speak to Marc.

'I'll see if he is in, Miss Manderly,' the man said, leaving her in the entrance hall while he went upstairs. It was obvious he was not used to having irate young women disturbing his normally serene, dignified environment.

Returning a few minutes later, he informed her that Marc would see her in the upstairs sitting room.

'Sara!' Marc greeted her joyfuly as she entered to find him surrounded by her paintings and sculptures.

Monica was there too, looking thoroughly perplexed. 'Miss Manderly,' she received Sara with a quiet smile. 'It seems that my brother is quite taken with your work, though I'm uncertain where we'll find space to place all of these.'

'There's no need to worry,' Marc assured his sister, continuing to move from one painting to another, examining each in turn and smiling broadly with appreciation. 'I don't intend to horde the whole lot. I'll give a few away to some of our closest friends. It will soon be the in thing to have a Manderly hanging in one's home.'

'That's what I've come to talk to you about.' Sara attempted to maintain an air of self-control, but her anger was too intense not to show.

'It would seem that Miss Manderly is upset with you, brother dear,' Monica remarked with an indulgent frown. 'And since I prefer to remain out of your personal squabbles, I hope you'll excuse me.'

'Of course,' Marc nodded indifferently at his sister's departure.

Pausing beside Sara, Monica said in a whispered aside, 'Don't be too rough on him. I'm afraid the tendency to go overboard when someone or something becomes important to us is an inherited family trait.'

Sara's anger faded a fraction. In spite of the jealousy she felt towards the woman, she had to admit that Monica had class. Someone else might have accused her of misleading Marc or being an opportunist. If Monica had such notions, she kept them well hidden beneath an exterior of graceful calmness.

Attempting to match her with the sister Marc described on their first encounter was impossible, but then Marc's view of the world was shaded by his eccentricities and one hundred proof Bourbon. 'I'll try not to,' she promised.

Monica nodded and closed the door on her way out to provide them with privacy.

'You can't buy up all my works!' Sara began as soon as she and Marc were alone.

'And why not?' he questioned with an innocent smile as he put down the painting he was inspecting and walked over to the liquor cabinet to pour himself a drink. 'They were for sale.'

'Yes, they were for sale, but . . .'

'All great artists had sponsors,' he interrupted. 'I'm sure I read that somewhere. Either that or they died destitute, and we can't have that happening to you. Therefore, I'll be your sponsor. You must understand the realities of life. Becoming a success doesn't rest on talent alone. There are hundreds of talented people out there waiting to be discovered,' he waved his arm in an expansive gesture before adding, 'Knowing the right people always helps.'

'I prefer to make it on my talent alone,' Sara returned firmly.

'In the end, you will,' he said, raising his glass in salute. 'I'm merely giving you a nudge in the right direction; bringing you out into the limelight, so to speak.'

'I want you to promise me that you won't buy any more of my work,' she insisted, refusing to relent.

'Not even if I fall madly in love with a piece?' he questioned woefully, placing a hand over his heart in a gesture of regret.

'Marc, please!' she sighed in exasperation.

'I love the way your mouth forms that little pout when you're frustrated,' he said, catching her chin to hold her face upwards.

Backing free of his touch, she frowned up at him. 'I'm serious about this.'

'All right, no more wholesale purchases,' he promised.

'And you'll return these?' With a sweep of her arm she indicated her paintings and sculptures scattered around the room.

'Absolutely not!' He shook his head in a negative gesture to emphasis his determination. 'I promised you a glass slipper, and I always keep my promises.'

'Glass slipper?' Attempting to follow his thinking was making her dizzy.

'The glass slipper was the key to Cinderella's freedom from a life of drudgery. Your success as an artist will provide you with the financial independence to achieve the same end. In other words, you can move out of Brad Garwood's kitchen.'

'My situation is quite a bit different from that of Cinderella,' she said, determined to make her point clear. 'In the first place, I'm independent. I get paid for my services. I have the choice of remaining or leaving to find other employment if the situation doesn't suit me. What you're offering me is a dependency, and a dubious one at that. Even if you were able to promote me into the "limelight", as you put it, for the rest of my life I could never be certain if it was my art people wanted or that they'd merely been duped into a fad and now so many people had so much invested they didn't dare let it die. With that question hanging over my head, I could never be happy. I can't accept a success based on someone else's manoeuvres.'

'All right, all right!' Marc held up a hand in a gesture of surrender. 'But I still refuse to return any of my purchases. I've grown much too fond of them.'

Shaking her head in exasperation, Sara started towards the door.

In two easy strides, he blocked her exit. 'What do you think about murals,' he questioned, smiling down on her playfully.

'Murals?'

'Yes, murals. I've been seriously considering getting a place of my own and I could commission you to do a mural or two for the walls. It used to be quite the rage.'

'I don't think so,' she refused.

'You could do anything you like; whatever suited your taste. I would even allow you to pick out the furnishings for the rooms to be certain they didn't clash with your painting,' he bargained.

'I don't think I want to take on such a large project right at this moment,' she hedged, her instincts warning her not to get mixed up with the Fallons.

'I'm not used to being so thoroughly rejected,' Marc smiled down on her charmingly. 'And I have to admit I find it a challenge.'

'I don't mean it to be one,' Sara replied, 'I'm simply trying to be honest with you.'

'Then I find your honesty refreshing, and I intend to get to know you better, Sara Manderly. Will you have dinner with me tonight?'

'I appreciate the offer, but the answer is no,' she refused politely but firmly.

'Think of it as a bribe to ensure my co-operation,' he suggested mischievously.

'In that case, the answer is an emphatic "no",' she frowned.

'Then think of it as Prince Charming attempting to make amends,' he revised the offer.

'You can make amends by not pulling another stunt like this again,' she said, moving around him to reach the door.

'Think of . . .' he began again, but she did not catch the rest of his words as she left the room, closing the door securely behind her. Eccentrics, no matter how charming or handsome or wealthy, held no interest for her.

'So far this day has gone from bad to worse,' she muttered during the drive home, adding, 'and worser,' as she turned the corner and spotted Margarete's silver Buick parked in front of the house. 'It has now reached horrible,' she amended with a groan as she pulled into the driveway and discovered Brad's car there too.

Inside, she found both of them upstairs in her studio.

'This bust of Mr Garwood is coming along marvellously,' Margarete effervesced.

'Thank you.' Sara forced a smile while mentally noting that effervescing was one of Margarete's true talents. The woman could make even the worst artist think they were a Picasso.

Although Brad remained silent, his expression one of studied politeness, Sara felt his hostility.

Margarete, on the other hand, seemed oblivious to it.

'You didn't say when you would bring more paintings over,' the woman continued. 'So I thought I would stop by and prod you with this cheque.'

Sara accepted the extended piece of paper. It was for a substantial sum, but that was not what made her hand shake as she shoved it into the pocket of her jeans. Brad was watching her closely and the colour of his eyes was darkening with each passing moment. 'Thank you,' she managed as Margarete smiled triumphantly.

'You're so lucky to have a Fallon for a sponsor,' the woman stated with a happy sigh. 'Now I must rush. Are these four paintings all right for me to take along?'

'Yes,' Sara confirmed. Then becoming mobile in an effort to escape Brad's gaze, she picked up two of the suggested works. 'I'll help carry them to your car.'

'It's been a pleasure to meet you, Mr Garwood,' Margarete extended her hand towards Brad. 'It's always a pleasure to meet anyone who's willing to help a struggling artist.'

'It would appear that Sara is not exactly struggling any more,' he returned coolly.

'I suppose not.' Margarete's smile faded somewhat as she quickened her exit. Outside, after carefully loading the paintings, she looked thoughtfully at Sara. 'It seems that your Mr Garwood is quite out of sorts over Marc Fallon's interest in you. I thought you told me that you and he had a business relationship.'

'We do,' Sara frowned. 'It's just that sometimes he forgets he's my employer and not my guardian.'

'I'm not so sure he sees himself in a guardianship role,' Margarete mused, forming her lips into a teasing pout.

'He's planning to marry Monica Fallon,' Sara offered as proof of her contention.

'Monica Fallon? My, my, that would put him right in the middle of Charleston society. Yes, it would be a very good move for a man in his position. The Fallon name carries a great deal of weight here. Which,' Margarete added, bestowing a hug on Sara, 'is why I'm so happy for you.'

'Don't expect too much,' Sara warned. 'I've spoken to Marc and told him that I don't want him manipulating my career.'

'My dear, giving an artist a push isn't manipulating their career,' Margarete admonished.

'I want to make it on my own,' Sara remained firm.

'Artists!' Margarete shook her head, then gave Sara a second hug to say she forgave her before climbing into her car and driving away.

'Are you going to tell me what's going on, or do I have to guess?' Brad's icy tones met Sara as she went back into the house.

'Obviously, you've already been considering the possibilities,' she snapped back, facing him defiantly.

'I'm not in the mood for games,' he growled. 'I want a straight answer.'

'You're merely my employer, not my guardian. Therefore I see no reason for me to account for the incidents in my life to you,' she threw over her shoulder, moving past him to enter the kitchen in an attempt to escape this confrontation.

'Do you want me to call Steve?' he threatened, following her and catching her by the arm. Swinging her around to face him, he added, 'I'm sure he would have a few questions.'

'There's nothing to tell.' She backed down a little. She didn't want Steve brought into this too. 'Marc simply bought all of my works that Margarete had in the gallery.'

'And why would he do a thing like that?' he questioned drily.

'Maybe he likes my work,' she retorted, flushing angrily.

'And maybe he's decided to play your angel. He'll distribute the pieces among his friends, keeping a few to display prominently in his own home, and very soon it will become the in thing to own a Sara Manderly painting or sculpture. Now tell me, what does he expect in return?'

'He doesn't expect anything! And he's not going to pull this kind of a stunt again,' she glared, brown fury meeting green ice as they stood practically toe to toe, both bodies tensed for battle.

'And how would you know that?' Brad raised a sceptical eyebrow.

'Because I've just come from his home. I told him I didn't want his help with my career and he agreed.'

'I detect a faint waver,' Brad noted sarcastically.

'Eccentrics are a little difficult to trust,' she hedged, refusing to tell him about the murals or Marc's attempt to bribe her into a date.

'I hope you keep that in mind. Marc Fallon can be very persistent and very charming when he sees something or someone he wants,' Brad warned bluntly.

Suddenly, uncontrollably, slow hot tears began to trickle down her cheeks as she balled her hands into tight fists. 'You don't think I'm any good as an artist!' she accused. 'That's what this is all about, isn't it? You don't think anyone could actually buy my paintings simply because they like them!'

Drawing an angry breath, he ran a hand through his hair. Then pulling her gently into his embrace, he smoothed her hair in a roughly caressing motion. 'That's not true,' he denied gruffly. 'I like your work very much. In fact, there's a painting upstairs I particularly want for my workroom. When I found out why Margarete was here, I told her it was already promised to me.'

For a moment, Sara considered struggling, but as the warm pressure of his chest moved in rhythmic breathing against her, the strange sense of belonging swept over her again. A mistiness clouded her mind and her sobbing began to subside. 'Honestly?' she stammered, bringing her hand up to wipe the tears from the cheek not resting against his shoulder.

'Honestly,' he replied, his arm tightening to hold her more securely. 'Now, I want you to promise me that you'll be careful where Marc Fallon is concerned. He's not the type of man you should associate with.'

His words brought her back to reality. Stiffening, she pushed away from him. 'Thank you for your concern, but I can take care of myself,' she flared, taking a couple of steps backward to place some distance between them. 'And if I need any further brotherly advice, I'll call Steve!'

'Sara,' he breathed her name warningly. For a long moment he stood staring at her indecisively, then he growled, 'I've got work to do,' and stalked out of the kitchen.

As soon as he was gone, her flush of anger turned to one of embarrassment as she reviewed her childish behaviour. How could she have allowed herself to dissolve into his arms in tears? What difference did it make whether or not he liked her work? He wasn't an expert on art. 'It's just been a very difficult day,' she muttered, still staring at the door through which he had passed. 'I would have cried over anything just to relieve the tension.' But even as she said this she knew it was a lie. Everything the man upstairs thought and felt made a difference to her. 'I've got to find a place to live tomorrow,' she sighed, 'before I make a complete fool of myself.'

Forcing herself into motion, she started towards her bedroom, only to come to a halt when she spotted Brad's wrist bandage lying on the counter. 'Men!' she snapped.

Wishing she didn't care so very much about this one particular male, she grabbed up the piece of elastic and stormed upstairs to his workroom. 'You're supposed to be wearing th . . .' she blurted out angrily, only to stop in mid-word as she reached his drawing board and saw the fresh bandage on his wrist.

'That one got wet when I was washing the dishes from breakfast,' he explained drily. 'I didn't feel like walking around feeling soggy all day, so I bought another. But I do appreciate your concern.' The 'even if you don't appreciate mine' was there in spirit.

'You should have left them for me,' she returned tightly, refusing to apologise for her earlier outburst.

'I'm not totally handicapped,' he frowned.

'Of course not,' she muttered through clenched teeth. Spinning sharply around, she started back out the door, but found herself pausing and turning back towards him. 'Did you get it wrapped correctly?'

'Good enough.' His manner was one of dismissal and she quickly took the cue and completed her exit.

Back in the kitchen, she slammed a few drawers and attempted to put the man out of her mind, but the effort was useless. Removing a roast from the freezer, she started to put it in the microwave to defrost, then remembered that this was Saturday.

Knowing that Brad might have other plans, she groaned as she realised that she was going to have to face him again. Marching stoically upstairs, she knocked, then hesitantly entered his workroom. He was still sitting at his drawing board, a look of anger mingled with frustration causing deep furrows to crease his brow. 'I apologise for interrupting you again,' she said, her voice softening in response to the tiredness evident in his eyes. 'But I was about to start dinner and it occurred to me that you might have other plans for this evening.'

'This is your weekend off,' he reminded her.

'I have to fix something for myself and I thought that if you were going to be at home, I would prepare dinner for the both of us. You could consider it an exchange for the breakfast,' she replied stiffly.

'I'll be staying home,' he conceded.

Nodding, Sara turned to leave, but with her hand on the door she glanced back over her shoulder to see him rubbing his forehead with his hand. The urge to return to him and massage his shoulders while trying to talk him into getting some rest was strong. But she knew he would not appreciate her interference. Stoically, she closed the door and hurried down the stairs.

The flowers began to arrive shortly after she had started dinner. The first arrangement was all red roses with a card from Marc begging her to forgive him. The second came fifteen minutes later and was yellow roses with a similar card. When the doorbell rang a third time, Sara made up her mind to put a stop to this.

'Please, take them back,' she told the delivery boy.

'I can't do that,' he said, his voice and expression

registering surprise that she would even make such a request. 'They've already been paid for.'

'All right,' she conceded. 'But this is the last. Agreed?'

'No, ma'am,' the boy shook his head apologetically. 'I have several more in the truck for you.'

'Several more?' Sara frowned.

'Yes, ma'am,' the boy smiled brightly, obviously impressed with his customer's extravagance.

'Then remove the cards and deliver the rest of them to the local hospital. Say they're a gift from an anonymous donor,' she directed.

'I can't do that. I'd lose my job,' he protested.

'Then bring them all in now,' she said with a resigned sigh.

'I can't do that either. Mr Fallon was very specific in his orders, and he's one of our best customers.'

'I don't believe this,' Sara muttered, as the boy nervously shoved the vase of flowers into her hands and tipping his hat hurried back to his van. She was still holding the new arrived arrangement of white roses when the phone rang. Picking it up, she was not surprised to hear Marc's voice on the other end of the line.

'Have you decided to forgive me?' he asked by way of a greeting.

'I told you this afternoon that you were forgiven as long as you didn't pull another stunt like the one this morning,' she said. 'Now will you please stop the flow of flowers.'

'First I want to know if you've forgiven me enough to have dinner with me,' he bargained.

'You're totally forgiven, but I will not have dinner with you,' she replied firmly.

'You're still mad at me for suggesting that you go out with me as a bribe,' he accused. 'I admit that was ungallant of me, but never mind. I hope you're not allergic to chocolates?'

Before she could make any response, the line went dead. Shaking her head, she carried the third bouquet into the kitchen. 'It's a good thing they're coming in their own containers,' she muttered, checking on the roast, 'or I'd be forced to arrange them in the cleaning buckets!'

Ten minutes later she was standing in the hallway with the fourth bouquet, pink roses this time, when the doorbell rang again. Opening the door with the intention of giving the delivery boy a piece of her mind, she was surprised to discover an elderly man standing on the doorstep.

'Are you Miss Sara Manderly?' he enquired politely.

'Yes,' she answered dubiously, her eyes falling on the large box the man was holding.

'Mr Fallon asked me to deliver this to you personally,' he smiled broadly, extending the beautifully wrapped package towards her.

Knowing from her experience with the florist's delivery boy that a rejection would only meet with failure, she smiled graciously. 'Excuse me just one moment,' she requested. Shoving the first two flower arrangements close together on the hall table, she placed the one she was holding next to them and accepted the box from the man.

'I hope you enjoy them,' he said with a pleased grin before walking away.

Closing the door, Sara stood staring at the gift. Whatever it was, it was heavy. Removing the wrapping, she discovered a five-pound box of a very expensive brand of chocolates. 'I didn't even know they made a box this big,' she mused.

'What's going on?' Brad demanded, coming down the stairs at that moment. 'Are we having an epidemic of . . .'

The words trailed off as he caught sight of the box in her hands and the three flower arrangements crowded together on the table.

'Apparently Marc Fallon still thinks I'm angry with him,' Sara explained tersely.

'To a bystander like myself it would appear that the man is attempting to do more than simply apologise,' he commented coolly. 'I hope you won't take this wrong, but I think your attitude towards his purchase of your paintings is a bit naïve.'

'I am not naïve,' she snapped, resenting the look on his face so reminiscent of Steve when he was about to point out that he had warned her and she had not listened. 'I've made it clear to him that no matter how many paintings he buys, I'm not for sale.'

'I don't think he's totally convinced,' Brad growled, indicating the candy and the flowers with his eyes.

'I can handle this myself, thank you,' Sara glared back.

'Then see if you can put a stop to these constant interruptions,' he requested acidly, as he retraced his steps back to his workroom.

'I'm trying,' she muttered under her breath. 'Men! They think they know everything!'

Marc called again a few minutes later and she again tried to reason with him. However, he continued to insist that only her agreement to go out with him would prove that he was forgiven. This she refused to do, and the flowers continued to arrive.

'This place is beginning to look like a mortuary,' Brad remarked icily, when she called him down to dinner. 'I thought I asked you to do something about stemming the flow.'

'Yes, master,' she muttered. Her nerves were wearing thin, and his obvious anger at a situation over which she had little control did nothing to help.

To make matters worse, the phone rang at that moment. Grabbing it up on the second ring, she immediately realised her mistake and wished she had gone into the kitchen and picked up the extension in there. It was difficult enough to remain somewhat civil to Marc without Brad staring at the back of her neck.

'Am I truly forgiven?' Marc asked for the umpteenth time.

Sara considered letting her temper go and telling him that she would never forgive him if he didn't stop the flowers immediately. Her intuition, however, warned her against this line of attack. His behaviour indicated that he would only find some other way of attempting to bribe her. Besides, she had to admit that it was flattering to have a man express his desire to see her in so flamboyant a manner. It would have been marvellously exciting if it was Brad who was sending the flowers. But it was not, and she had to come to some agreement with Marc before his attentions became an unbearable embarrassment. 'I've told you several times that you're forgiven,' she replied.

'Then you will have dinner with me?' he repeated his bargain.

Glancing over her shoulder, Sara caught Brad's expression of disapproval. Suddenly the image of Monica Fallon flashed into her mind and in a moment of defiant, jealous anger, she did the one thing she had promised herself she would not do . . . she accepted the invitation. The atmosphere in the room immediately became charged with tension.

'I thought we would go to the Sunday evening dinner and dance at the yacht club,' Marc was saying in pleased tones. 'I've been dying to see you in a proper dress. You do own a regular dress, don't you?'

'Yes, I own several,' she responded, forcing her voice to sound light while feeling as if a two-ton weight was pressing against her.

'Something slinky and low-cut,' he suggested hopefully.

'Something demure and practical,' she returned, wanting desperately to retract her acceptance but unwilling to admit her mistake under Brad's intense scrutiny.

'Oh, well, I guess I'll have to settle for what I can get,' Marc lamented, then added, 'But to be perfectly honest, I would have settled for taking you in a gunny sack if necessary. I find you so very exceptional.'

Sara remained silent, a lump building in her throat. Why couldn't Brad be the one who found her so very exceptional? Instead he preferred Monica Fallon, with her great beauty and even temperament.

'I'll be by to pick you up at six-thirty,' Marc continued.

Chiding herself for even thinking of Brad, Sara's back stiffened as she said with forced cheerfulness, 'I'll be ready.'

'I thought you had better sense,' Brad growled even before the receiver clicked into place.

'You said you wanted me to put a stop to the flow of flowers,' she reminded him bitingly.

For what seemed like an eternity but was, in reality, only a couple of minutes, he studied her in cold silence. Then through clenched teeth he said, 'I'm going for a walk,' and slammed out through the front door.

The moment he was gone, a wave of terror swept over Sara. Pride, the fear of appearing foolish, nothing, could keep her from running after him. As she fell into step beside him, he raised a questioning eyebrow.

'I didn't think you should go walking alone,' she said defensively. Then as his expression became black, she wished she had made even a dumb excuse rather than telling him the truth.

'You're not my bodyguard,' he snarled. 'I thought I'd made that very clear.'

'And you aren't my big brother,' she retorted, lowering her voice as they passed a couple of tourists who were wandering along the quaint side street.

Slowing his pace so that she didn't have to jog to keep up with him, he said in quieter tones, 'No, I'm not, but if I were I would take you over my knee and spank you.'

Throwing him a hostile glance, she would have liked to have parted company with him, but her instincts would not allow her to desert him. The feeling of terror had passed as soon as she had joined him, but she knew it would return if she left his side. 'Could we go back to the house and eat dinner before it gets cold?' she suggested tightly.

They had come to a corner. It was obvious he had planned to cross the street and continue towards the park. Hesitating, he glanced towards her and with a resigned sigh nodded in agreement. Changing direction, he began to retrace his steps back to the house. 'Don't you ever think before you act?' he demanded in a low grumble, breaking the prolonged silence between them.

'I used to think before I did anything,' she muttered, then added, 'But lately, I seem to be suffering from a mild form of insanity, and it appears to be getting worse rather than better.'

'Once people discover that Marc Fallon made an extensive purchase of your paintings and then they see you out with him, they're going to think you're his mistress or, at the very least, that you're using him to further your career,' he persisted grimly.

She knew he was right and was almost ready to admit it

when an uneasy prickling sensation on the back of her neck caused her to glance towards the street. A white Lotus passed them and she recognised Monica at the wheel. Jealousy sparked a fire of defiance. They were almost back at the house and she quickened her pace as she said sarcastically, 'That should prove interesting. Once people find out that I've been your housekeeper and that Marc has decided to become my self-appointed sponsor, they won't know who to link me with. Of course there's always the possibility they'll link me with both of you. That would be enough to gossip about for years. Just think, in two weeks time, without ever having slept with a man, I'll have become one of Charleston's most infamous femme fatales!'

Kicking the door closed as they entered the house, Brad grabbed her by the shoulders and spun her around. 'This isn't a joking matter!'

'Who said I was laughing?' she retorted, twisting out of his grasp and stalking off towards the kitchen.

The evening did not improve. Brad remained stoically disapproving, while Sara vacillated between going out with Marc and calling him and breaking the date. It wasn't that she wanted to go out with him. In fact, she disliked the idea more and more with each passing minute. However, her practical side knew that attempting to break the date would be an act of futility.

Marc's tenacity, if his behaviour today could be used as a measure, was quite strong. He would, no doubt, park himself on her doorstep, which would only lead to further hostilities. As she saw it, the most reasonable solution was to go out with him this one time and make it perfectly clear that she was not interested in seeing him again.

## CHAPTER SEVEN

ON Sunday morning, Sara attempted to regain some normality in her life by following her usual routine. She went to church with Helen, Steve and the children and ate brunch with them afterwards. The effort, however, was not a total success. Ida's name came up several times, and although Steve and Helen refrained from alluding to Sara's present housing arrangement in front of the children, an air of strain existed among the adults.

Finally, when the two women were alone in the kitchen washing the dishes, Helen's reserve broke and she asked bluntly, 'What do you intend to do? Steve mentioned that you promised him you'd be out of Brad Garwood's home by the end of the week. Is that still your plan?'

'I'll be out by the middle of the week,' Sara assured her, adding apologetically, 'But that may mean moving in here with you and Steve for a few days or even a few weeks.'

'We'll love having you,' Helen said, her tone expressing relief. 'But I'll have to put you in with Joanie. Ida will have to have the guest room. The children get on her nerves and she needs a place to be alone.'

'And the rest of the family needs a break from her too,' Sara added what Helen was too polite to say and the other woman smiled in agreement. 'Did she say how long she would be here before going on to Florida?'

'No, but I suspect she'll stay at least two weeks.'

'I admire the ease with which you're taking all this,' Sara sighed. 'To tell you the truth, the thought of all of us being sequestered in the same house for two weeks with the possibility of Brad Garwood's name coming up and the children spilling the beans is enough to give me the hives!'

'I think the only viable solution is to tell her right off that you were the man's housekeeper for a few days,' Helen stated firmly. 'Joanie was quite taken with him and regularly mentions the picnic out at The Pines. Also, for some reason, she keeps trying to explain that you're living at Brad's house but not with him. The only problem is that sometimes it comes out backwards, and I wouldn't want that version to be Ida's first knowledge of the situation.'

'Agreed,' Sara nodded, adding wistfully, 'I'm certainly glad one of us is able to think straight these days.'

'I've noticed that you haven't exactly been yourself, lately,' Helen commented, pausing while putting a cup away to take a good long look at her sister-in-law. 'You know, I don't believe I've ever seen you like this before. You've always been so in control of your life and your emotions. But lately you've been edgy and maybe even a bit unstrung.'

'True,' Sara flushed.

Helen pursed her lips in thoughtful consideration while she continued to study her sister-in-law. Then breaking her silence she said, 'It's Brad Garwood, isn't it? You've fallen for him.'

'I'm hoping it's just a passing insanity,' Sara admitted grudgingly. 'And please, whatever you do, don't tell Steve.'

'You have my word on that,' Helen promised, then asked in a concerned tone, 'And how does Brad feel about you?'

'Part of the time he treats me like a kid sister who's in need of a great deal of guidance,' Sara grimaced distastefully.

'And the other part?' Helen persisted.

'Like he can't stand to have me around,' Sara muttered, the pain showing in her eyes.

'Then the man's a fool,' Helen declared, giving Sara an encouraging hug.

'And you're prejudiced,' Sara forced a smile. 'A condition for which my ego is very grateful.'

'Maybe you're mistaken about how he feels,' Helen suggested.

Sara shook her head. 'He's interested in Monica Fallon.'

'Steve did mention something about that,' Helen admitted with a sympathetic frown. 'It was in connection with a ball, if I remember correctly.'

'I'd rather not talk about this any more,' Sara requested. 'Besides, I have to be off. I'm spending the afternoon apartment-hunting. With any luck, you won't have the entire Manderly clan under your roof at one time.'

'I know you,' said Helen, her motherly manner becoming strong. 'There's more to all of this than you've admitted, but I won't press. Just don't forget that I'm here when you feel the need to have someone to talk to.'

'You wouldn't believe it anyway,' Sara shook her head sadly. 'I'm beginning to think of it as a family curse.' Then before Helen could probe further she left.

She hadn't told either Helen or Steve about Marc Fallon's large purchase of her paintings or that she had a date with Marc. It was a cowardly thing to do, but she knew that they would have disapproved and Brad's disapproval was almost more than she could handle. She didn't need any added pressure.

Her afternoon's search turned up two possibilities, but neither of them would be available until the end of the next month.

Brad was sitting at the kitchen table drinking coffee and reading the Sunday paper when she returned. 'Find anything?' he asked as she came in.

'Nothing that's available soon enough,' she sighed tiredly. 'Looks like I'll be moving in with Helen and Steve for a while.'

He nodded his acceptance of this solution, making no further attempt to persuade her to remain in a custodial position in his home. Obviously, he had reconsidered the situation and decided that to remove her completely from his life would be the best arrangement for all concerned.

'Would you like me to fix you something for dinner before I leave this evening?' she asked, changing the subject.

'I'll be dining with Monica, so that won't be necessary,' he replied, only a slight deepening of the green of his eyes betraying his continued disapproval of her date. 'However, I would appreciate it if you would rebandage my wrist after I shower. I'm driving and although it feels much better, it's still a little weak.'

'Of course,' she agreed, a wave of anxiety sweeping over her and making her feel suddenly extremely exhausted. 'If you'll excuse me, I think I'll go and rest for a while before I dress. It's been a long day.'

'Perhaps, if you're so tired, you should consider staying at home this evening,' he suggested.

For a moment she considered making him a bargain . . . she would remain at home if he would remain home too. Then realising how ridiculous that would sound, she simply threw him a disgruntled frown and went into her room. Lying on the bed, staring at the ceiling, she wished she had the nerve to ask him not to go out. Then in a wave of honesty, she was forced to admit that she wasn't certain if her anxiety was because she truly sensed that he would be in danger or because she knew he would be going out with Monica Fallon and her jealousy was affecting her.

A slow tear trickled from her eye, running down her cheek past her ear to melt into the pillow beneath her head. She had always believed that one day she would find a man she could love, it had just never occurred to her that he might not love her.

'So much for fairy tales,' she muttered, forcing herself off the bed and into the shower.

She had just finished blow-drying her hair when Brad knocked on the bedroom door. Pulling on a robe in place of the towel in which she had been sitting, Sara stepped into the kitchen.

He was dressed in slacks and a short-sleeved white cotton shirt. A thick shank of brown hair, still damp from his shower, hung down across his forehead. Without thinking, she reached up and brushed it back, then flushed at the forwardness of her action as his eyes darkened.

Clearing her throat nervously, she said, 'This will be easier if you'll sit down.'

Following her suggestion, he seated himself at the kitchen table and as she pulled a chair near and sat down too, he extended his arm in her direction.

The intoxicating scent of his aftershave assailed her senses, making it difficult for her to concentrate on what she was doing. As she carefully manoeuvred the bandage around the wrist and hand, the feel of his skin spread a warm glow through her and an atmosphere of intimacy began to envelop them.

Suddenly Brad broke the silence that had been between them since she had begun to work the bandage into place. 'You're not wearing a damn thing under that robe,' he growled accusingly. Startled, she glanced upward into his darkened features. But before she could speak he added, 'Why didn't you tell me you weren't presentable? This could have waited.'

Feeling suddenly very vulnerable, Sara realised that it had seemed perfectly proper to be in his presence whether she was fully clothed or unclothed. Flushing, her startled expression hardened into a defensive glare. 'You've been behaving so much like Steve, I guess I finally bought your big brother role,' she snapped. A heavy silence followed. Angry embarrassment kept her hands steady as she completed fastening the bandage. Finally slipping the last clip into place, she said tersely, 'There. How does that feel?'

'Fine,' he returned, pushing his chair back and rising. Then standing, towering over her, he added darkly, 'As you've been so quick to point out, I am not your brother, and in future I would appreciate it if you would keep that thought in mind.'

The flush that had never quite left her face deepened as she met his shuttered gaze for one painfully intense moment before he turned and stalked out of the room.

Back in her room, as she applied her make-up, she tried to force her enigmatic employer out of her mind, but his presence continued to linger. And in spite of his hostile exit she could not erase the sensation of intimacy she had experienced as they had sat at the table. Even though she was fighting her emotions every step of the way, the man was becoming more and more a part of her and she knew that never seeing him again was going to be like cutting off an arm or a leg. Still, that would be easier than seeing him with someone else.

The dress she had chosen to wear was one of her favourites. It was a light-weight, multicoloured creation of blues, pinks and purples with a form-fitting bodice, discreet neckline and puff sleeves. The full, tiered skirt was knee-length and had a gently flowing motion to it when she walked.

Angry with herself for allowing Brad to affect her so adversely, she wasn't paying attention as she began to fasten the zipper, and three-quarters of the way up her back it caught in her slip and stuck. Pulling and tugging did nothing to help. It would move neither up nor down. 'This is all his fault,' she muttered, glaring at the ceiling as if she could see through the other two floors into his bedroom. A muscle in her back went into a spasm, forcing her to realise how very tense she was about this evening.

Too emotionally overwrought to even attempt to sort out what was going on inside of her, she concentrated on the zipper. 'Darn!' she fumed, going into the kitchen and hunting through the drawers for anything that looked as if it would be useful.

When that search proved futile, she went up to her studio. Maybe one of her tools would offer a solution. In her unruly frame of mind, she knocked a can of paint-brushes to the floor, and they hit the wooden surface with a loud clatter.

'What's going on in here?' Brad demanded from the doorway, his voice filled with exasperation.

'Sorry I disturbed you,' she threw back, setting the brushes on the table with almost as loud a noise as they had made when they had fallen.

'Don't you think you should finish zipping your dress?' he remarked bitingly as if he found her appearance disgraceful.

'That's exactly what I'm trying to do,' she snapped back. 'It's stuck, and I thought I might find something in here to help.'

For a moment he stared at her as if in indecision, then with a resigned sigh he said, 'I could use some help myself.

I can't get my tie to look right. How about an exchange? I'll fix your zipper and you can tie my tie.'

Recognising this as the most practical solution for both of them, Sara reluctantly agreed.

'Your zipper first,' he directed, his manner tightly controlled as he turned her around.

His breath played havoc on the sensitive nerve endings in the back of her neck while his hands brushing against her skin, felt so very enticing. She bit her lip and prayed he would be finished soon.

'You're going to have to help,' he growled after a few minutes that had seemed more like a lifetime. 'Hold the dress tight below the place where this zipper is stuck.'

Immediately obeying, she felt the fabric come free and Brad finished fastening the dress. A sigh of relief escaped from her as the disturbing contact was broken. Turning around to thank him, she found herself uncomfortably close to his large frame and backed away half a step.

'What would you have done if I hadn't been here to help?' he questioned drily.

'I would have been forced to wait until my date arrived and asked him for his help,' she replied coolly, determined to maintain an outward air of indifference.

'Then I'm glad I was here,' he scowled. 'I wouldn't want Fallon getting any more ideas than he already has.'

Briefly, she considered reminding the infuriating man that he had only recently told her to remember that he was not her brother and adding that she would appreciate it if he would keep that thought in mind. However, not wanting to increase the hostilities between them and not fully trusting herself about what she might reveal, she bit back her retort and turned her attention to his tie. 'I don't know how to make one of these knots,' she frowned. 'You'll have to guide me through it.'

As she stood following his instructions, the sensation of intimacy she had experienced earlier returned with an even greater intensity. A vague fogginess clouded her mind and she saw herself and Brad as a comfortably married couple preparing to go out for the evening. The urge to go up on tiptoe and playfully kiss away the downward tilt at the corners of his mouth was strong. Then the image of Monica Fallon impinged into the misty illusion and harsh reality returned. Almost violently she shoved the knot into place. 'There, that should do it,' she announced, taking a step backward as she spoke and intending to continue her flight without hesitation.

But Brad caught her hands before she could turn away from him. 'Sara, don't,' he began, only to stop himself in mid-sentence as if it was necessary to reconsider his words. His fingers toyed with the small ring on the little finger of her left hand as the pause lengthened perceptibly.

Not trusting herself to meet his gaze, Sara concentrated on the middle button of his shirt.

'Sara,' he began again, his hold on her hands tightening, 'don't let Marc drive you home if he drinks too much.'

Her body went taut. She had been so certain he was going to make a very different request. Then realising that this was merely wishful thinking brought on by her fantasies, she pulled her hands free. 'I'm not stupid and I don't need your guidance to behave rationally,' she told him with a cool calmness she did not feel.

'Sara,' he breathed her name with an exasperated sigh.

Glaring up at him defiantly, her eyes dared him to give her any more advice.

'You look very lovely,' he murmured.

'Thank you,' she stammered, her expression softening in confusion.

'You're welcome.' His voice caressed her as his hand came up to stroke the line of her jaw. A stillness enveloped them; a stillness so intense that it created the illusion that they were the only two people in the world.

As a wistfulness replaced the confusion in her eyes, his thumb travelled over her lips and they parted as if to whisper, but no sound came out.

Green jade flamed and his fingers entwined themselves in her hair. Her breath locked in her lungs as his head inclined towards hers. The thought of fighting him did not enter her mind. The need to be touched by him was too strong.

But before his lips found hers, the harsh sound of the doorbell intrusively reverberated on the air, shattering the illusion of isolation. As if suddenly becoming aware of his actions, Brad straightened away from her, his hand falling to his side and his expression darkening.

'Brad?' she said his name quietly, questioningly.

The bell rang again. 'Marc sounds impatient,' he commented, his cool exterior fully in place once again.

Sara's mouth tightened into a hard line. Spinning round, she descended the stairs without a backward glance.

'You look absolutely delicious,' Marc greeted her. Then as he handed her a florist's box containing a wrist corsage made of white rosebuds, his eyes travelled over her shoulder and he added, 'Evening, Brad.'

'Evening, Fallon,' Brad returned the salutation in censorious tones.

Sara knew without a doubt that he had followed her downstairs to check on Marc's condition, and she bristled. With Steve she would have tolerated such an invasion of her privacy, but with Brad Garwood she would not. 'The flowers are lovely,' she smiled at Marc. 'If you'll excuse me for a moment, I'll get my bag and we can be on our way.'

'She does move nicely; an enticing yet gentle sway to the hips, don't you think, Brad?' Marc commented with an air of masculine appreciation as she walked swiftly away from the men.

Missing Brad's response as she let the kitchen door swing closed behind her, Sara frowned darkly. Marc was deliberately baiting the other man, and it made her angry. Marc's little games might be basically harmless, but they placed other people in difficult or embarrassing situations, and she was tiring of him rapidly.

Suddenly her back muscles tightened as the anxiety she had been experiencing lately returned. 'Brad Garwood can take care of himself,' she stated sharply to the image in her bedroom mirror, and with that pronouncement she rejoined the men.

Following a short, stilted salutation, she and Marc left. As she walked beside her escort to his car, she could feel Brad's eyes on her but refused to acknowledge his presence.

'I had the impression that at any moment Brad was going to ask me how much I'd had to drink before I came to pick you up,' Marc quipped as they reached the small yellow sports car.

'How many have you had?' she questioned, a slight edge to her voice.

'Only two since lunch. You have a very sobering effect on me, lovely. However, since I'm led to believe that the modern, independent female prefers to be in the driver's seat, why don't you chauffeur us?' he suggested, extending the keys towards her.

'I'm not so independent that I always insist on being in the driver's seat, but I've always wanted to drive a

Jaguar,' she said, accepting the offer with relief and, admittedly, a twinge of delight.

After giving her some brief instructions, Marc settled back in his seat and proclaimed with a laugh, 'This is marvellous!'

'Being chauffeured?' she questioned as she switched on the engine and the machine began to purr, causing a spark of excitement to flash in her eyes.

'Having pleased my princess and in the process put off the angry dragon,' he clarified with an amused look.

'Put off the angry dragon?' She threw him a puzzled glance.

'You didn't think Brad was actually going to let you leave with me behind the wheel?' he laughed, turning to wave to the man standing in the doorway.

'He does have a strong brotherly instinct,' Sara frowned, using anger to mask the pain.

'Is that what you call it?' Marc mused, more to himself than to his companion. Then in stronger tones, he said, 'I don't like the idea of you still living under his roof.'

'It's a job,' she replied, then wondered why she didn't tell him that she was planning to move fairly soon.

'It makes me furious to think of you waiting on him hand and foot,' he glared as she guided the car out on to the main road.

'I do not wait on him hand and foot,' she frowned, 'and I would appreciate if we could change the subject.'

'All right.' Marc smiled mischievously. 'Let's talk about you waiting on me hand and foot. Or better still, why don't I hire someone to wait on both of us hand and foot and we can spend our time simply enjoying each other's company.'

'I refuse to wait on anyone, nor do I wish to be waited on myself,' she scowled. 'What I would like is not to discuss anything more personal than the weather while I concentrate on my driving.'

'As you wish,' he conceded. 'But I warn you, I plan to get you out from under that man's roof.'

Knowing that Marc would insist on having the last word and again rebelling against divulging her plans to him, Sara offered no comment to this last statement. Instead she glanced at the sky and said, 'It looks as if it will stay clear tonight.'

'And you'll look ravishing in the moonlight,' Marc declared gallantly, smiling at her resolve to change the subject while refusing to keep the conversation strictly impersonal.

Arriving at the club, Sara discovered that the sobering effect he had professed that she had on him was short-term. As soon as they were seated he began to drink.

To make matters worse, the sense of dread she had been experiencing where Brad's safety was concerned had returned. It was not as strong as it had been the night of the accident or the afternoon before, but it was there, causing her to feel edgy and tense.

The waiter was bringing Marc his third before-dinner cocktail when Sara felt a prickling sensation on the back of her neck and intuitively knew that Brad was in the room.

'Good evening, Miss Manderly, Marc,' said Monica as she and Brad paused at Sara and Marc's table on their way to their own.

'Good evening, Miss Fallon,' Sara returned, sensing a hidden anger in the woman and guessing that Monica's understanding nature was wearing thin. The woman could not have missed seeing her and Brad together the day before and she might have got the impression that they were out for a pleasant stroll together which would not fall into the category of proper relations with the hired help. Or perhaps Marc's courtship of an obscure painter was not sitting well with the Fallon household.

'Evening, Monica, Brad,' Marc raised his glass in salute, then drained the contents.

Brad merely nodded, his expression grim.

'I do hope you're not going to over-indulge and embarrass all of us tonight,' Monica reprimanded gently.

'How unkind of you to say such a thing!' Marc's hand went to his heart. 'Especially in front of a lady I'm trying so very hard to impress.'

'I apologise, dear,' Monica leaned down and kissed his cheek. 'But sometimes you can be trying.'

'I have heard that women consider men with faults to be challenging,' Marc quipped. 'That should give me quite an advantage with the ladies over paragons such as Brad.'

Sara's eyes darkened cynically, but she held her tongue. Marc's behaviour was embarrassing enough without her entry into the fray to offer a few indiscreet insights into Mr Brad Garwood's character.

Glancing at the object of her silent hostility, black ice greeted her and as if he could read her mind, Brad said drily, 'I have my faults, but I prefer not to advertise them.'

'Now I've been properly chastised,' Marc sighed. 'That calls for another drink.' Turning slightly sideways, he raised a hand to signal the waiter.

Monica threw her brother a perturbed glance, then turning towards Brad said, 'I believe our table is ready.'

'Yes,' he agreed, his disapproving gaze shifting from Marc to Sara.

'I hope you have a pleasant evening, Miss Manderly.' Monica forced a strained smile as the waiter appeared to take Marc's order.

'And I hope the same for you,' Sara returned, determinedly avoiding meeting Brad's eyes a second time.

'Don't let Monica upset you,' Marc winked mischievously as the other couple moved out of earshot. 'She's still a bit snippy about the ball.'

'You mean about the railing coming loose? I'm sorry if I dampened the party,' Sara said, then as an even more horrible thought occurred to her she demanded anxiously, 'She hasn't recognised me, has she?'

'No, she hasn't recognised you, and as for the railing, while I found it to be the highlight of the evening, it was an inconsequential occurrence to my sister ... Except, of course, for the sudden loss of Brad's presence for a period of time.'

As Marc spoke, Sara glanced past his shoulder in the direction in which Monica and Brad had departed, only to discover that they were now seated at a table not far away. To add to her discomfort, Brad was positioned directly in her line of vision. At the moment, he was smiling at something Monica was saying, and she pulled her attention back to her escort as a sharp stab of pain hit somewhere near her heart. If she couldn't get hold of herself, she was going to have to leave Charleston. Feeling snippy herself, she said with a touch of acid, 'Then I don't understand why Monica is upset. I thought all the guests seemed to be enjoying themselves.'

'But it was not at Cyprus Point,' said Marc, pitching his voice a couple of octaves higher in an effort to mimic his sister. Then in more normal tones he added with grudging admiration, 'And you wouldn't believe the concessions people were willing to make to please Hanna.'

'Concessions?' Sara questioned.

'The night of the ball only candlelight and torches were allowed in the grounds at Cyprus Point,' he started to elaborate, then paused as the waiter came to take their orders for dinner. It wasn't until after the man was gone that he continued. 'As you might have guessed, that was a fire hazard. As a consequence the local fire department provided a truck and men who sat out there all night in case they were needed. Of course they had to be parked out of sight because only horsedrawn vehicles were allowed within visible range of the house. The guests had to park their cars in the meadow near the gate and wait to be transported to the ball in carriages Hanna had hired for the occasion. And then there were the costumes. Can you imagine grown men and women allowing themselves to be bullied by an old lady for fear of being permanently excluded from her segment of society?'

'It would seem,' Sara noted drily, her gaze travelling back to the table where Monica was holding court as nearly every guest present paused dutifully to greet her, 'that your grandmother was not the only Fallon people are willing to treat with deference.'

'True,' he agreed, a spark of admiration lighting his eyes as he too turned to look in his sister's direction. 'Sometimes I actually feel sorry for Brad.'

Sara's jaw tightened and she forced her attention back to her own table. 'Your family still owns Cyprus Point. Why didn't Monica have the ball there this year if it was so important to her?'

'Our father wouldn't allow it.' Marc's expression darkened, as if he was suddenly haunted by ghosts from the past. 'He hates Cyprus Point. Or more accurately, he hated his mother and the place reeks of her. You see, old Hanna never approved of Monica's and my mother. She badgered her constantly, telling her she wasn't good enough to bear a child of Halloway blood. After one of their more heated confrontations, my mother went driving to blow off steam and died in a car crash. My father never forgave Hanna and refused to set foot in Cyprus Point ever again.'

'If there was so much hatred between your grand-mother and your father, why did she leave the plantation to him?'

The waiter arrived with their salads and Marc waited until the man was gone before answering. 'She had no choice,' he said, dipping a piece of cold boiled shrimp into the hot cocktail sauce.

'Didn't have a choice?' Sara frowned.

'My grandfather knew that Hanna loved Cyprus Point as deeply as my father had loved my mother. As a punishment for the accident or maybe because he knew that Hanna had only married him to keep Cyprus Point, he set up his will so that my grandmother had the use of the place during her lifetime, but on her death it would automatically go to my father. Still, Hanna tried. She knew my father would sell the place as soon as she was gone so she worked on Monica and me. She tried to make us love the place as much as she did.'

'And do you?' Sara questioned between bites of shrimp.

'Not with old Hanna's ghost hanging around.' A crooked smile curled Marc's mouth. 'I think that's really the reason Father refused to allow Monica to have the ball out there this year. He didn't want any more ghost stories to circulate. Last year one of our guests swore she saw Hanna standing at the top of the stairs admiring the proceedings. Of course, the woman had been at the champagne all evening and even her own nose was a fog to her. Still, it did cause quite a stir.'

'And what about Monica? I gather she's still very attached to the place.'

'Yes, Hanna had a great deal more success there. My

sister is obviously even willing to marry a Yankee in order to retain the family home.'

The chiding quality in Marc's voice provoked Sara. 'Marrying Brad Garwood isn't a sacrifice,' she retorted, then wished she had held her tongue as Marc's eyes flashed. He had laid a trap and she had fallen into it.

During the remainder of the meal, she kept the conversation on less personal ground. Marc insisted on having champagne with the main course and drank nearly two full bottles, while Sara had three glasses. This was one more than her usual limit. But the flash of green from the table beyond, combined with a continuing sense of anxiety, caused her to imbibe a little extra with the hope that it would help her relax. It didn't.

'I'm not in the mood for dancing,' Marc announced, as the waiter cleared away their dishes. 'Why don't I take you for a moonlight cruise on our yacht?'

'I don't think so,' she rejected the offer. The man's speech was slurred and she doubted whether he could negotiate the room, much less navigate a large vessel.

'I insist on at least showing it to you. It's my favourite toy.' He was rising. Not wanting to create a scene, Sara smiled demurely and followed.

Amazingly, he managed to move through the crowded room without incident. As they left, she saw several large and medium-sized yachts moored along either side of a long, wide wooden pier. A breeze was blowing in over the water bringing with it the tangy smell of the ocean.

'I really think we should be going home,' she suggested as he guided her along the plank surface.

'After you see *Wandering Lady*,' he remained adamant, retaining a firm grip on her arm.

'Marc, where are you going?' Monica's voice sounded from behind them and Sara breathed a sigh of relief.

It was, however, a shortlived relief as Marc pivoted her round and she came face to face with Brad's angry scowl and Monica's less than kind frown.

'Surely you and Miss Manderly were not planning to go for a sail?' Monica questioned disparagingly.

'My dear sister, may I remind you that we're both past the age of consent.' Marc's manner was deliberately provocative, and Sara flushed.

'You're in no condition . . .' Brad growled.

'No Yankee is going to tell me what condition I'm in!' Marc interrupted. Releasing his grip on Sara, he balled his hands into fists and drew his arm back.

Anticipating the blow, Brad blocked the punch with his forearm, inadvertently causing Marc's forcefully delivered swing to change direction and catch Sara in the eye. Losing her balance, she staggered backwards. Suddenly there was nothing solid beneath her feet and she was falling. Black depths enveloped her as she hit the water and went under. Coughing and spluttering, she surfaced to find Brad in the water beside her forcing a life-preserver into her arms.

'Is she all right?' Monica was calling from above. 'Shall I go for help?'

'I'm fine,' Sara managed to choke out, not wanting a crowd of people summoned to witness her humiliation.

'Sara, I'm truly sorry,' Marc apologised from the pier.

'Next time I'll remember to duck,' she muttered.

'There won't be a next time,' Brad growled, guiding her to a ladder Monica had lowered from the yacht.

Minus her shoes, which were now at the bottom of the harbour, Sara managed to climb to the deck with Brad close behind. Her dress clung like a second skin, leaving very little to the imagination, but she was past embarrassment.

'Here, let me wrap this round you,' Marc insisted as she reached the deck. Producing a blanket, he carefully arranged it around her shoulders. 'And I really do apologise.'

'I think you'd better get Miss Manderly an ice pack for her eye,' Monica instructed as she handed Brad a duplicate blanket. 'It looks as if it's beginning to swell.'

Holding the blanket securely around herself, Sara tenderly touched the area near her eye. Monica was right: it was tender and it was swelling. Too humiliated to cry, she simply stood silently wishing she could melt into the deck.

'Luckily this fell on the pier.' Monica handed Sara the purse that matched the lost shoes. 'And I also want to apologise for my brother's behaviour. I don't know what's got into him lately. He's never been violent before.' Although her manner was polite, she could not completely hide the distaste with which she viewed the proceedings, and Sara couldn't blame her.

Marc returned momentarily with an ice pack and a brandy. Sara accepted the ice pack but refused the drink.

'It will help remove the chill,' he encouraged.

'I just want to go home and take a warm shower,' she said as firmly as her shivering body would allow.

'Since I'm in no condition to return to the dance, I'll take Sara home,' Brad stated, his manner holding no compromise.

'I brought her here. I'll see her home,' Marc glared.

'No,' Monica interjected before a new scene could develop. 'I'll drive you home, brother dear, and put you to bed before you can do any more damage.' There was an authority in her voice that quelled any further protests Marc might have been considering.

As the foursome walked towards the parking lot, Brad

fell into step next to Monica. 'I'm sorry the evening had to end so abruptly,' he apologised.

'It wasn't your fault,' she returned, flashing her brother a look of pure fury.

Stepping on a sharp object, Sara breathed in sharply to stifle the cry of pain that threatened to escape.

Glancing down, Brad seemed to realise for the first time that she was barefooted. Barely pausing, he swung her up over his shoulder with his good arm.

'Put me down!' she snapped, her entire body scarlet with indignation.

'Stop squirming,' he ordered. 'With my sprained wrist, this is the only way I can get you to the car safely.'

'I've always suspected that there was a great deal of caveman in Yankees,' Marc muttered.

'Be quiet!' Monica admonished, and no more was said by anyone before they parted company.

However, as soon as Sara and Brad were in his car and on their way home, he was quick to break his stoic silence. 'What in the hell did you think you were doing going down on the pier with that man?' he demanded.

'Don't curse at me,' she retorted. 'And I wasn't going down there willingly—he was dragging me. But I wouldn't have got on the yacht!'

'How in the world did you survive this long on your own?' he growled.

'I was doing just fine until I became associated with you and your friends,' she returned hotly.

'Marc Fallon is not one of my friends.'

'Monica is,' she pointed out sharply, then feeling snippy she added, 'even if you are an uncultured Yankee.'

'Sara!' His voice held a warning note and she retreated into silence, wishing she had held her tongue.

Arriving back at the house, she was out of the car and on

her way to the door before he had turned off the engine.
She wanted to give him no chance to pick her up again in
his most unceremonious fashion.

Dropping the ice pack in the kitchen sink, she went
straight into her bedroom and discarding her soggy
clothes, climbed into the shower. The sense of security she
experienced in this house, combined with the soothing
water and the remaining effects of the champagne she had
consumed, took the edge off of her nerves. By the time she
climbed out of the shower, she was beginning to feel
almost relaxed until she caught sight of herself in the
mirror. A dark circle was already starting to form around
her eye. Groaning aloud, she blew her hair dry. Then
dressing in a light, short nightgown, she pulled a robe on
over it and went out into the kitchen to fix herself a fresh
ice pack.

Brad, showered and dressed in a fresh pair of slacks and
a knitted pullover, sat at the kitchen table. He rose as she
emerged and moved towards her. 'Let me see what damage has been done.'

Knowing that to refuse would be useless, she turned in
his direction and his face darkened. 'I should have slugged
Fallon,' he scowled.

'Please, not while I'm in receiving distance,' she requested.

'Sit down and I'll fix you a fresh ice pack,' he directed,
continuing to look grim.

Ignoring his orders, she continued towards the refrigerator. 'I can fix my own ice pack.'

Throwing her an exasperated glance, he left the kitchen
only to return in a moment with two glasses of brandy.
'Drink this,' he said as she finished shoving ice into a
plastic bag.

'I'm not much of a drinker,' she protested with a frown.

'It will help settle your nerves,' he persisted, taking her arm and leading her to the table.

'My nerves are just fine,' she argued weakly, the touch of his hand having a disquieting effect on her entire body. 'All I need is a little sleep.'

But when she tried to pull loose he retained his hold and seated her in one of the chairs. 'I need you to re-bandage my wrist,' he pointed out, indicating the bandage lying on the table as he seated himself in a neighbouring chair.

His nearness made her tense and she took a sip of the brandy. 'Did the salt water hurt your stitches?' she asked, attempting to quell the heady sensation the feel of his flesh produced as she worked the bandage around his arm and hand.

'No,' he murmured, his uninjured hand coming up to tenderly touch her cheek just beyond the bruising.

Stiffening away, she took another sip of the brandy as his hand dropped back on to the table. Clearing his throat, he said, 'I have a confession to make.'

Glancing up, Sara met green velvet looking down on her. 'A confession?' she stammered, taking yet another sip of the brandy.

'Until tonight, I have honestly always believed you were, at least a brown belt in karate.'

'Are you trying to tell me that I'm no good as a body-guard?' she quipped, taking a healthy swallow of the brandy. The warm liquid was not only beginning to taste very good but was producing a lovely, relaxed state of being.

'Not unless you learn to duck,' he drawled.

'You know, we look like two refugees from a bar-room brawl,' she mused, reaching out to stroke his jaw with the tips of her fingers. It was such a nice jaw.

'Does your eye hurt much?' he questioned gruffly, catching her hand and placing it back on the table.

'A little,' she admitted, finishing the brandy, then running the tip of her tongue slowly over her lips.

His features stiffened as the velvet green of his eyes took on subtle deep overtones.

'You could kiss it and make it better like my grandmother used to do,' she suggested. Then, shocked by her words, she pressed a hand against her forehead. 'I didn't mean that.'

Pushing his chair back, Brad walked over to the cabinet and extracted a bottle of aspirin. Taking out two, he ran a glass of water, then carried the pills and water to the table where Sara sat still wondering what had caused her to lose control like that and make such a ridiculous request. 'Take these,' he directed, and she did. After which he said, 'And now it's time for you to be in bed.'

'I agree.' Nodding to emphasise her words, she was suddenly caught in a wave of dizziness. To make matters worse, when she tried to stand, her legs refused to work properly. Sinking back into her chair, she had an overwhelming urge to giggle. She knew her condition was not the least bit funny, but she giggled anyway, then felt like a complete fool.

'I've never seen one glass of brandy go to a person's head so fast,' Brad muttered.

'One glass of brandy and three glasses of champagne,' she corrected, adding with a petulant pout, 'I told you I wasn't much of a drinker.'

'And you were right. You certainly can't hold your liquor,' he frowned. 'I'll have to remember that in future.'

'We don't have a future,' she mused, a wistful sadness coming into her eyes. 'You and Monica have a future. You're going to marry her and spite Hanna by having little half-Yankees running around Cyprus Point.'

'You shouldn't listen to gossip. Monica and I are good

friends and nothing more,' he said. 'Now stand up and go to bed.'

'You're not going to marry her?' she glanced up hopefully.

'No. Now stand up,' he demanded sharply.

'I'm not sure I can,' she confessed, flushing embarrassedly as another giggle surfaced.

'After tonight I can see why Steve is so protective of you,' he grumbled, helping her into a standing position by placing his hands under her arms to steady her.

'I resent that!' she glared.

'I know you do,' he sighed in exasperation. Then wrapping his good arm around the tops of her legs, he again hoisted her on to his shoulder. This time she did not protest but simply hung limp for the short trip into her bedroom. Coming to a halt beside her bed, Brad leaned down and placed her in a standing position in front of him.

'Thank you,' she murmured, looking up into his face with her one good eye while continuing to hold the ice pack over the other.

'You're welcome,' he responded gruffly.

'I've never had a strange man in my bedroom before. Not that you're strange . . .' She bit her lip and her brow furrowed as she searched for a remedy to her remark.

'I know what you mean,' he growled, 'Steve made it very clear to me. Now it's time for you to go to bed.'

'You feel so nice,' she sighed, ignoring his instructions as she moved her hand upward over his chest to slip beneath the collar of his shirt.

'Lady, you may not have a brown belt, but you are dangerous.' His voice was a low grumble as he unfastened the knot of her robe and slipping the garment off, tossed it on to a chair. 'Now get into bed.'

A petulant pout formed on her lips. 'Only if you'll kiss my eye and make it better. You're partly to blame.'

'I'm not to blame,' he frowned.

'Yes, you are,' she argued.

'If you promise to go directly to bed, then I'll kiss it,' he bargained tightly.

'Promise,' she smiled mischievously, dropping the ice pack on the bed and sliding her other hand up around his neck too.

Capturing her hands, Brad placed them down by her sides. Then holding her by the upper arms, he leaned down and lightly kissed her eye.

'It hurts here too.' She indicated a spot on her cheek.

Frowning, he kissed the spot.

'And here.' She pointed to the bridge of her nose.

Closing her eyes, she swayed against him invitingly as he bent to kiss this latest professed site of pain. Then because she could not resist, her arms circled him and her hands splayed out over his back to delight in the solid feel of him.

'I suppose the whole side of your face hurts,' he murmured, a huskiness entering his voice as he trailed kisses down her nose to discover her lips parted and waiting. But he did not immediately accept the invitation. First he placed tiny kisses at the corners of her mouth, then kissed each lip separately.

'You have a very medicinal touch,' Sara smiled, raising up on tiptoe to add her strength to the contact.

His breathing became ragged as his hands travelled down her sides to halt possessively on her hips. The fabric of her nightgown seemed non-existent beneath his touch as every curve of her body moulded to his with an intimacy she had never before known.

Then abruptly, he straightened and capturing her arms

unwound them from his body. Before her disorientated mind could react, he had set her down on the bed, removed her slippers, lifted her legs on to the mattress and covered her with the sheet. 'Now go to sleep!' he barked, and stalked out of the room slamming the door behind him.

For what seemed like an eternity Sara lay, barely breathing, her body rigid in her state of humiliation and self-directed anger. Then the tears began to flow. How could she have offered herself to him so wantonly? She had certainly made a complete fool of herself this time. Brad might not be planning to marry Monica, but he also did not want her cluttering up his life.

# CHAPTER EIGHT

SARA awoke the following morning with a splitting headache to the sound of male voices arguing in the kitchen.

'I thought I'd made it perfectly clear that I didn't want anyone following me around!' Brad's angry tones were distinct.

'After the accident I felt it was necessary. You could have been set up,' Steve pointed out, his tone matching that of his employer.

'Since no further accidents have occurred, I think we can safely assume that it was merely a coincidence that the truck pulled out when it did,' Brad growled.

'You're probably right.' Steve's voice was black. 'But about last night . . .'

'What about last night?' Brad interrupted caustically. 'If your man has eyes he knows I wasn't the one who knocked your sister into the water. I was the one who dived in after her.'

'What the hell was she doing out with Fallon in the first place? Everyone knows the man's a drunkard and not to be trusted.'

'And exactly how do you propose I was to stop her? Lock her in her room? I'm in a restricted position!'

'You could have called me!'

'And what would you have done? I don't think Sara takes too kindly to being told what to do and who to do it with.'

'Whether she likes it or not, I'm taking her home with

166

me until she finds a place of her own,' Steve announced with finality.

'Yes, that would be for the best,' Brad's voice was hard.

Groaning, Sara pulled the sheet more securely around her and choked back the new flood of tears that begged to be released as the memories of last night returned with a painful vividness. Alone in her room she flushed with embarrassment at her remembered wantonness and humiliation at Brad's rejection.

The ringing of the phone interrupted any further exchange between the men. She heard Brad answer it and after a few moments say, 'Sara will be fine except for a black eye.' This was followed by a longer pause, after which he said in indulgently polite tones, 'If you feel that strongly, of course I'll come.' Then as the receiver clicked into place, his voice returned to its formerly hard level as he addressed Steve. 'That was Monica. She wants me to meet her at the yacht club and I don't want one of your men following me. Is that understood?'

'You're the boss,' Steve conceded in a disgruntled tone.

'Try to keep that in mind in the future,' Brad growled as he slammed out of the room.

Sara rose slowly, her head pounding violently with the increased elevation. Dressing in jeans and a tee-shirt, she gave Brad time to leave the house before she emerged into the kitchen.

'Sara, you look dreadful!' Steve greeted her with harsh concern as he rose and moved towards her.

'Could you whisper?' she requested in hushed tones, her hands going up to hold the sides of her head.

Leading her over to a chair, he found two aspirin and after getting her to swallow them, poured her a cup of coffee. 'You're acting more like you have a hangover than a black eye,' he frowned, tilting her head back to examine the purple discolouration tinting her face.

'I have both,' she groaned, freeing herself and taking a sip of the coffee. It had the effect of swallowing acid. An intense feeling of anxiety swept over her, but in her present state she had trouble dissociating it from the pain.

Scowling, Steve walked over to the refrigerator and found some tomato juice.

'Could you walk a little softer,' she muttered, holding her head propped up on her hands, her elbows resting on the table. 'Now that I know what a hangover feels like, I don't understand why anyone would do this to themselves more than once.'

'Here, drink this.' He pushed a glass filled with a red concoction in front of her.

'It's awful!' she protested after taking a cursory sip.

'So is your condition! Drink it!' he commanded.

'Whisper, please,' she pleaded, attempting to swallow the whole thing in one gulp.

'That should help.' He shook his head ruefully.

'How, by taking my mind off my head and directing it towards my stomach?' Sara snarled.

'About last night . . .'

'I refuse to discuss last night,' she interrupted.

'I can't believe you let yourself drink too much. Especially when you were out with a lush,' he reprimanded, ignoring her interruption.

'I didn't drink too much when I was out with Marc. Your boss gave me a brandy when we got home. It was that on top of the champagne that did it,' she muttered.

'He didn't take advantage of you, did he?' Steve demanded.

'I asked you to keep your voice down—and no, he didn't. He's not interested in me.' The chimes from the front door bell suddenly split the air and she moaned as the sound reverberated in her brain.

Shaking his head in abject disapproval, Steve left to answer the summons. Again, angry male voices filled the air, then Marc Fallon burst into the kitchen with Steve close behind.

'Sara, I'm so sorry,' he apologised, approaching her and tilting her head back for a better view of the injured eye. 'I'm afraid jealousy brings out the worst in me.'

'Apology accepted, provided you keep your voice down,' she bargained, recalling her own irrational responses to this unhappy emotion.

'I didn't know salt water could cause a hangover,' he frowned.

'Brad gave her a brandy after they returned home,' Steve explained in a grumble.

'He didn't take advantage of you, did he?' Marc demanded.

'No, he didn't,' she snapped back, wondering if that was all the male population thought about. Steve's remedy was beginning to take effect and although she was physically better, a stronger and stronger sense of impending disaster was building within her.

'I think you should go back to bed,' Marc advised, 'you look even paler than when I came in.'

'No . . . something is wrong,' Sara shook her head trying to clear the fog.

'Are you sick?' Steve was immediately by her side, feeling her forehead.

'No, it's not that.' She brushed his hand away. 'I can't explain why, but I have the same sort of feeling I had the night of Brad's accident. Something terrible is going to happen—I know it.'

'He's at the yacht club with Monica Fallon,' Steve frowned. 'What could happen there?'

'I don't know, but Monica could be in danger too.' Sara looked beseechingly up at Marc.

'I never question a woman's intuition,' he smiled. 'Come on, I'll drive you out there.'

'I'll just tag along behind,' said Steve, following them outside and climbing into his car.

'Thank you,' Sara murmured as she seated herself next to Marc. She felt decidedly foolish. But then again, she had been behaving foolishly for the past week.

'Do you have these types of premonitions about people often?' he questioned, an amused tilt to his mouth. 'Because if you do, you could start writing one of those psychic columns predicting disasters.'

'This isn't a joking matter,' she frowned. Then as an acute wave of anxiety swept over her, she added, 'And could you please drive a little faster?'

'Getting arrested won't get us there faster,' he pointed out, his expression taking on serious overtones as he realised she was in earnest.

By the time they reached their destination, her head was clear of its earlier fog and her whole concentration was focused on her instinctive knowledge of impending danger.

As she and Marc walked into the clubhouse, Steve joined them. The clerk at the front desk gave all three a curious glance before his attention came to rest on Sara's eye. She did not even flush, as her anxiety built to monstrous proportions.

'Have you seen my sister?' Marc demanded.

'She and Mr Garwood went down to the yacht a few minutes ago,' he replied, unable to drag his gaze away from Sara's face.

Immediately she was on her way out the door and down to the pier with the men close behind. Her pace had turned into a sprint, forcing them into a jog.

'Hey, Bobbie, retie those lines,' Marc called out to a young boy ahead of them who was busily unwrapping the heavy lines mooring one of the boats.

'But your sister wants to take *Wandering Lady* out,' Bobbie looked towards the approaching trio in some confusion.

'Tie her back up,' Marc ordered. 'I want to check her out. There may be something wrong.'

'What's going on? Marc, what are you doing here with Miss Manderly?' Monica demanded from the deck above them.

'Permission to come aboard, skipper,' Marc called up, already ascending the ladder to join his sister, with Sara and Steve close behind him.

'What is this all about?' Monica frowned as the three completed boarding while Bobbie retied the lines. 'I thought we agreed at breakfast that I could have the yacht today.'

'We did, and I apologise for the intrusion,' Marc smiled sheepishly. 'But apparently, in addition to painting, Sara's into premonitions, and she seems to think that you and Brad are in some kind of danger. So I thought I should check out the engine before you get out into the ocean and have no way of getting back.'

'Really!' Monica muttered as her brother disappeared below deck. 'I don't believe any of this.'

Sara's face reddened in embarrassment, but still the sensation of danger was too strong to allow her to desert her conviction that something was very wrong.

'Speaking of Brad, where is he?' Steve asked, his eyes travelling over the empty deck and bridge.

'I think the first question to be answered is who you are,' Monica frowned.

'I'm Steve Manderly, Sara's brother,' Steve introduced himself. 'And I work for Brad Garwood. The desk clerk said he was here with you, but I don't see him and it's important that I locate him. Do you know where he is?'

'The man was exhausted,' Monica explained, obviously annoyed by this invasion of her privacy. 'I persuaded him to take the day off and go fishing with me. He's in one of the cabins napping right now. I was going to wake him in an hour or so.'

'You know,' said Sara, forcing a calmness into her voice she did not feel, 'I've never been on such a large vessel before. You don't mind if I look around, do you?'

Before Monica could protest, she was past the woman and on her way below deck to the cabins. The first one was empty, but in the second she found Brad stretched out on the double bed. He appeared to be sleeping peacefully. Sara paused, her rational side waging a battle with her intuition. Intuition won. No matter how foolish she looked, she couldn't let him go out on this boat today. Walking stiffly over to the bed, she shook his arm gently. When his eyes didn't open, she shook him again, this time harder. Panic began to build when there was still no response. 'Please, wake up,' she stammered.

'Sara, what's wrong?' Steve demanded, entering the cabin and joining her by the bed.

'I can't wake him,' she choked out, touching Brad's face caressingly. 'Do you think he's had a heart attack?'

'No,' Steve frowned, placing his hand over the pulse in Brad's neck. 'His heartbeat is slow but strong and his breathing is regular.' Raising an eyelid, he looked at the pupil and his jaw hardened. 'I'd say he was drugged.'

'I've checked the engine and there's nothing wrong

with it,' Marc's voice sounded from the passageway before Sara could react to Steve's diagnosis. A moment later he entered the cabin and coming to a halt beside her, demanded, 'What's going on?'

'We can't wake him,' she said, fighting back the tears. 'You'd better call an ambulance.'

'That won't be necessary,' Monica announced calmly from the doorway where she had been silently observing the others. 'He'll wake up in a couple of hours or maybe a little longer. I had to compensate for his size and might have made the dose a little heavier than I'd planned. But he's in no danger right now. I don't plan to have him die from an overdose of drugs.'

'You . . .' Sara turned to face the woman, only to have her next words catch in her throat as she saw the gun in Monica's hand.

'Yes, Miss Manderly, me.' Monica's expression was ice. 'And it would appear that you and your brother are much too nosy for your own good.'

'Monica, what's got into you?' Marc demanded, staring at his sister in disbelief.

'Sorry, baby brother. I didn't want to get you mixed up in this,' she said remorsefully. 'But I have to take care of Brad today. Hanna will never forgive me if I let those papers be signed. Can you imagine a Yankee owning Cyprus Point? Of course, I would have preferred to marry him first and get the property out of Daddy's hands, but Brad, apparently, isn't the marrying kind.'

'You aren't making any sense,' Marc tried to reason with her.

'I'm making very good sense and you know it.' Her voice was chillingly calm. 'When old Mrs Collins died just before signing the papers it was obvious Hanna was serious about never letting the property out of our hands.

Of course, Martin Sayford was a different problem.' Her mouth formed a petulant pout. 'I waited for Hanna to do something about him. But when the week before the papers were to be signed arrived and she still hadn't acted, I realised that she was counting on me.'

'Counting on you?' Marc muttered.

'Yes, counting on me. It wasn't so difficult either.' A wild gleam sparked in Monica's eyes. 'The man was a drunken bore. He agreed to meet me in the mountains for what he thought was going to be a very enjoyable weekend—as if I would have let someone like him touch me! He told his wife he was going fishing with friends. I had him rent a cabin with the stipulation that it had to be secluded. I told him I didn't want his wife finding out and causing a scene. Then I got him drunk and challenged him to a race. He was so sloshed he could barely get into his car, much less negotiate those mountain roads.'

'Give me the gun,' Marc directed.

'I can't do that,' she refused. 'I'll need it to convince these people they have to abandon ship after we're out in the ocean.'

'You can't be serious,' he admonished.

'I think she's dead serious,' Steve observed darkly.

'You, Mr Manderly, are a very perceptive man,' she smiled approvingly. Then directing her attention back to her brother, she said, 'Since I don't think I can trust you to co-operate, you'll have to stay locked up in here with the others until we're out of the harbour. But you're a Halloway and I know you'll stand by me when the time comes.'

'We are not leaving this harbour.' Marc moved slowly towards his sister. 'You're going to see a doctor. You need help.'

'Careful, Fallon,' Steve cautioned in hushed tones.

'She won't harm me, will you, Monica?' Marc continued his progress across the tiny cabin.

'I don't wan't to,' she admitted, a faint waver of indecision in her eyes. 'But I can't fail Hanna. You know how angry she can be. You even tried to warn Brad the day after the accident, but he wouldn't listen.'

'I was only putting on a show to impress Sara,' Marc frowned. He was now directly in front of his sister and holding out his hand, ordered, 'Give me the gun.'

Monica made a negative gesture with her head.

'Hanna is dead. She can't be angry with anyone,' he tried to reason with her.

'You'd better not say things like that. Hanna will hear you,' she warned. 'Now step back, I want to close this door and lock it.'

'You can't honestly want to kill three innocent people because of an old woman's ravings,' Marc scowled, standing his ground.

'I have to, don't you see?' A plaintive quality entered Monica's voice as she once again wavered. 'Hanna will never forgive me if I don't save Cyprus Point from outsiders.'

'Hanna is dead! She can neither forgive nor not forgive,' Marc stated forcefully. 'Besides, killing Brad and the others won't help you keep that damned plantation. After you left this morning, Dad told me that if anything happened to stop the sale this time, he was going to turn it over to one of the historical foundations and let them do with it as they wished.'

'No, he can't!' Monica shrieked.

'He can and he will,' Marc assured her.

Frustration mingled with dispair played over the woman's features. 'Hanna's going to be so angry,' she muttered, her control slipping. Then looking into her brother's face, she asked pleadingly, 'Will you protect me from her?'

'I promise, I'll protect you,' he said.

The gun dropped to the floor as she dissolved into tears in his arms.

While Marc soothed the sobbing woman, Steve quickly retrieved the gun and slipped out of the cabin. Sara knew he had gone to call the police and an ambulance. Sinking on to the edge of the bed, she picked up one of Brad's hands and sat holding it tightly, trying to stop her trembling.

'My manners!' Monica suddenly pushed away from her brother and dried her eyes. 'We have guests and I haven't even offered them a drink. Miss Manderly, could I get you something? Some iced tea, perhaps?'

'That's not necessary,' Marc assured her in humouring tones. 'You've been under a lot of strain. Why don't we go to the next cabin and you can lie down.'

'Absolutely not! Guests can't be neglected,' Monica admonished him. 'That's a sign of bad breeding. Now, Miss Manderly, what can I get for you? A brandy, perhaps?'

'No, nothing. But thank you,' Sara forced her voice into a polite mode, not wanting to throw the other woman into yet another mood change.

The sounds of several pairs of feet could now be heard above them and Monica's attention shifted to the new arrivals. 'It seems as if we have several guests topside,' she said. 'I'd better see to them.'

Marc led her away while Sara continued to sit clutching Brad's hand.

The paramedics arrived only moments later and she was forced into a corner while they examined him. 'He'll be fine,' the older of the two men assured her as they transferred his still unconscious form on to a stretcher. 'His heartbeat is strong and his blood pressure is good. Don't you worry.'

She nodded, unable to speak from the strain of holding back her tears. Once the men were gone, she allowed herself a few minutes alone, then drying her eyes, went up on deck to join the others.

Her 'premonition of disaster' story earned her a few guarded glances, but Monica's behaviour garnered the majority of attention. Between bouts of offering everyone drinks and being solicitous towards Sara's eye, she calmly explained to the police about the necessity of keeping her family home. She told of manipulating Martin Sayford and arranging accidents for Brad as if these were rational everyday activities like pulling weeds from a garden.

Taking Sara aside, Marc apologised for his sister's behaviour.

'It isn't your fault she's sick,' said Sara, adding, 'We all owe you our lives.'

'I have to believe that in the end she wouldn't have gone through with murdering all of you,' he shook his head sadly. 'I only hope the doctors can help her bury Hanna once and for all.'

'I hope so, too.' Sara soothed.

'Does Brad know what a lucky guy he is?' he questioned, reaching out to take her hand.

'I think we should rejoin the others,' she suggested tightly, freeing her hand and moving back towards Steve.

'The man's a fool,' he muttered, following her.

After some quiet discussion between Marc, Steve and the police, it was agreed that the police would escort Monica to a private sanatorium where she would be held under guard until the District Attorney could decide what charges to bring against her. Marc remained with her, holding her hand and telling her that everything would be fine. She accepted the solution calmly, placing her faith in her brother's words.

Standing in the parking lot, watching the police drive away with Marc and Monica, Steve offered to drop Sara off at his house, but she insisted on going to the hospital with him. She had to see Brad one last time to be certain he was really all right.

'Have you been having these premonitions long, Sis?' Steve asked as he guided the car out on to the main road.

'Only where the family are concerned,' she replied quietly.

'Like Mom,' he said. It was more of a statement than a question.

She nodded but remained silent. Knowing her well enough to understand that she was not ready to talk about this yet, he said no more.

Arriving at the hospital, the doctor told them that Brad was going to be fine. 'He had a pretty large dose, but he's fighting the drug. He's been drifting in and out of consciousness and it's going to take some time before he can work all the barbiturate out of his system.'

'Can we see him?' Steve questioned.

'For a moment,' the man agreed.

'What happened?' Brad questioned, opening his eyes to discover Steve standing beside the bed. 'They won't tell me anything in here. The last thing I remember is drinking a cup of coffee on the yacht and then feeling so dizzy I had to lie down.'

'That coffee contained quite a wallop,' said Steve, then added with a grin, 'It's good to see you back in the world of the living.'

'Wallop?' Brad muttered, his expression one of confusion.

'You were drugged,' Sara clarified softly. As he shifted his gaze until she fell into his line of vision, she could see how hard he was struggling to remain conscious. Her jaw hardened as she had to fight to keep herself from reaching out and touching him.

Frowning, he shifted his gaze back to Steve. 'Drugged? Why?' he demanded.

'Monica turned out to be a little unbalanced. She was planning to deep-six you to save the family estate,' Steve explained. 'She was also the woman who called you the night of the accident and drove the truck that pulled out in front of you. She'd even rigged the railing on the balcony the night of the ball. She'd planned to lure you out there and somehow manoeuvre you into leaning against the thing.'

'That was a pretty risky way to stage an accident,' Brad muttered. 'In fact both of them were.'

'That's what made her so difficult to spot. She was willing to take risks you wouldn't expect a murderess to take,' Steve frowned.

'How did you know I was in trouble?' Brad questioned, furrowing his brow in an effort to remain alert.

'Sara had a premonition.' Steve glanced at his sister with a playful gleam in his eye. 'I'll bet you never guessed she was psychic on top of all her other abilities.'

'Nothing about Sara would surprise me,' Brad murmured, losing his battle to remain awake and drifting back into unconsciousness.

Swallowing hard, Sara caught Steve's arm. 'I think we should be leaving,' she said, pulling him out of the room. Brad's words had stung, reminding her of what a fool she had been where he was concerned. She could not face him again.

'Why don't you throw a few things into your suitcases

and finish packing tomorrow?' Steve suggested as he drove her back to Brad's house a few minutes later. 'You look tired.'

'I'm fine,' she refused his suggestion. 'They'll be keeping Brad in the hospital tonight and part of tomorrow and I want to use this opportunity to pack and move out.'

'Mom's arriving soon. You're not going to change your mind and decide to stay around to nurse him for a few more days, are you?' he questioned.

'No, I'm not going to remain to nurse him,' she assured him tightly.

'Get some rest before you start packing,' he advised as he dropped her off.

'I will,' she promised.

Alone inside the house, she wandered from room to room as if saying goodbye to a much loved, long occupied dwelling. There was too much pain for tears. Fighting to retain control of her emotions, she directed her body's nervous energies into packing. It was an unorganised muddle as she threw things into boxes and suitcases, but at the end of two hours she had successfully moved all her personal things out of the bedroom and bath.

Cramming the last box into her car, she realised that she was too tired to trust herself to drive to Steve's. Besides, being perfectly honest, she had to admit that she wanted this one last night in this house. Too tense to lie down she climbed the stairs to her studio.

The clay bust stood on its stand in the centre of the room. Unwrapping it, she ran her fingers over the roughly defined features. A shudder shook her, but she refused to allow herself the luxury of tears. Brad was going to live; that was all that was important.

Somehow she had to free herself from the bond she felt towards him. Maybe distance was the answer. She would go to Paris. All painters should go to Paris at least once during their lifetime, she reasoned philosophically. With the money in her savings account and the cheque from the gallery for the work Marc had purchased, she had enough to live on for quite a while. She might even find a job teaching English. That had been her second major in college.

A small voice within her warned that distance would do no good, but still she was determined to try. She couldn't remain in Charleston. Even if she managed not to run into Brad, Steve would be a constant reminder of him.

She noticed a lone painting leaning against one wall. Without question, she knew it was the one Brad had set aside for himself the day Margarete had come by to pick up the pieces for the gallery.

Carrying it into his workroom, she placed it on his drawing board. 'It's a gift,' she told the emptiness around her. 'Something to remember me by.' Then in muted tones she added, 'I only wish there were gifts to forget people by!' She lingered in the room only momentarily. Brad's presence was much too strong in there. Without closing her eyes, she could almost see him standing at the window or sitting at his drawing board.

Back in her studio, she stared at the clay head. There was no reason to cover it. She knew now that she could never finish it.

Exhaustion overwhelmed her and curling up on the couch, she fell into a fitful sleep.

It was dark when she awoke. Turning on to her back, she saw the moon and stars shining through the skylight. 'A night for lovers,' she murmured in her grogginess, then hated herself for the thought.

The remembered plan to go to Paris returned and her expression hardened. She knew the voice inside was right

... distance would do no good. But she had to try something, anything, to break the tenacious hold Brad had over her.

Thinking back, she realised that it had begun when Steve had first shown her the photograph of the green-eyed man. Staring at the face peering out at her from the piece of celluloid, she had found herself recalling every scrap of conversation she had ever heard regarding Brad Garwood. At the time she had convinced herself that her interest was purely an artistic fascination with his features.

Pressing her hand over her mouth, she fought the urge to shout out that the fates were cruel. How could she be so emotionally linked to a man who found her presence an irritation? Life was so unfair!

The sound of footsteps on the stairs brought her abruptly into a sitting position, and glancing at the luminous dial on her watch, she saw that it was a little after eleven. A spasm of fear shook her. It wasn't a fear of the man approaching. She had no doubt as to his identity and knew that he would not harm her. It was a fear of herself and how she would face him.

His form blocked the doorway as he came to a halt and stared into the moonlit room. Sara sensed more than saw the rigidness which came over him when he realised that he was not alone. There was a click and the room was suddenly flooded with light.

'Sara,' Brad growled her name. 'Your room downstairs was empty. I assumed you'd be at Steve's house.'

'I was too tired to drive,' she said tightly. 'Didn't you see my car?'

'I didn't come in through the back. I came by taxi and the driver let me out in front,' he replied stiffly.

'I'm sorry if I surprised you,' she apologised, licking her

lips nervously under his scrutiny. 'I didn't expect you to come home tonight.'

'I checked myself out of the hospital.'

He hadn't moved from the doorway and the tension in the room was increasing steadily. 'Do you think that was a good idea?' she questioned, running a hand through her dishevelled hair.

'I've slept off the drug.' He seemed to be studying her, as if searching for something.

Awkwardly, she rose. 'I should be going now.' She meant her voice to sound calm, but the tone was terse and his expression darkened. 'I'll finish picking up my things tomorrow while you're out signing the papers on Cyprus Point.'

'I won't be signing those papers,' he said curtly. 'I've talked to David Fallon. Considering the circumstances, he's agreed to let me out of the agreement with no penalties.'

'I'm sorry about Monica,' she managed to get the words out in a level voice, still not certain that Brad had not been in love with the woman.

'Me, too. I thought she was a friend. I knew she was upset about her father selling the family estate, but I thought I could convince her that I would care for the place as much as she did.'

'And that was why you were seeing her?' The question came out before Sara realised what words were forming and a flush reddened her cheeks.

Some of the tautness left his stance. 'Yes. That . . . and to keep an eye on you. I didn't want you going out with Fallon. When I couldn't stop you, I arranged to be around in case you needed help.' His mouth formed a hard line as his gaze fell on her eye. 'Obviously my caution was well founded.'

'Marc saved your life . . . our lives,' she said, feeling that she had to defend the man after what he had done.

'Does that mean he's now your hero?' Brad demanded acidly.

'No, I was only trying to be fair,' she sighed, swallowing the hard lump in her throat. 'Please, I don't want us to part in anger.'

'No,' he agreed, his manner softening.

'Now, I really must be going.' She started resolutely towards the door, but still he did not move.

'I'm still a bit foggy about what happened, but I seem to recall Steve saying something about you having a premonition.'

'It was just one of those nuances of fate,' she muttered.

'Tell me,' he persisted, 'did you have one of your premonitions the night of the ball?'

'No . . . yes . . . sort of. I didn't know what it was. I only knew that I felt compelled to go,' she confessed tightly.

'I take it, then, that you don't have these kind of things often.'

'No, not often.'

He was watching her closely while continuing to block her exit. 'It must be distracting to have total strangers disrupting your life.'

'Normally I only have reactions to members of my family. You're the first . . . stranger.' Glancing away from the intense green of his eyes, she added, 'And now I really must be going.'

'I want to thank you properly for the part you played in saving my life. I'll come by to take you to breakfast tomorrow and we'll discuss it,' he said, moving aside to let her pass. 'What time will you be ready?'

'A simple "thank you" will suffice,' she fought back the tears. 'I'll be much too busy tomorrow to see you.'

'But I insist.' His voice held no compromise.

Swinging around to face him, her chin came up defiantly. 'I don't want your gratitude—I haven't got time for it. I've decided to go to Paris. All artists should go to Paris.' She tried to force a lightness into this last sentence, but it fell flat. Angry at herself, she resumed her flight.

'Damn it, Sara! You're not going anywhere.' Brad caught her by the arm. 'At least not until I've had a chance to talk to you.'

'Please!' She felt her control slipping and knew she could not stand up against one of his brotherly routines or, even worse, a pledge of friendship brought on out of gratitude.

'I'm not going to lose you, Sara. Not without a fight,' he growled.

There was a desperation in his voice that caused her to look up into his face. 'I don't understand,' she stammered.

'I promised your brother that as long as you were under my roof I would not make any advances towards you, and although it's been nearly impossible at times, I've tried to keep that promise. But now . . .'

'You promised Steve what?' she interjected.

'He had a right to ask—he's your brother. And at the time, I was so angry with you, I felt certain I would have no trouble keeping my word.' His voice softened as his hands came up to cup her face. 'I was such a fool.'

'Fool?' The word came out barely above a whisper.

'The night of the ball when I held you in my arms, I'd never been so aware of a woman. And later, even with the impression your landlady had given me, I couldn't force you out of my mind. You continued to haunt me until I wanted you so badly I was willing to pay any price to have you.'

'I remember,' she murmured, as his hands left her face

to circle behind her, drawing her to him to add emphasis to his words.

'I've never believed in love at first sight,' he continued, tightening his hold as if he was afraid she might attempt to slip away. 'I've always thought that two people had to take time to know one another before a long-lasting bond could be established. I refused to consider the possibility that I was already in love with you even after you entered this house and it suddenly felt like a home. Then there was that first morning when you came out of your room with your hair all mussed and your eyes still foggy from sleep . . .'

'You growled at me,' she accused, 'and made me feel like an Ugly Duckling.'

'Only because you looked so inviting I could barely stop myself from taking you in my arms and wishing you a very improper good morning.' He kissed the bridge of her nose. 'And I was locked into that promise I'd made to Steve. You have to believe that I never wanted to be rid of you. I only wanted you out of my home so that I could court you.'

'To be certain that what you felt was really love and not just lust?' she questioned, fear glistening in her eyes.

'No.' He looked hard into her face, to allow her to read the depth of his emotions. 'I love you. I don't need any time to be certain of that. I feel as if you're a part of me that's been missing all these years.' Feathering kisses over her face, he captured her lips for a kiss that spoke of an unquenchable hunger. Straining against him, she let her body tell him of her own need of him.

Deserting her mouth, he nibbled along the cord of her neck, causing goosebumps to rise on her sensitised skin. When she responded with a low moan of pleasure he asked huskily, 'Can I assume that if I were to ask you to marry me, you wouldn't tell me this time that I'm being ridiculous?'

A glimmer of the pain he had experienced at her earlier refusal flashed in his eyes, startling her by its intensity. 'That's a reasonable assumption,' she replied, kissing the hollow of his neck.

'Woman, I wonder if you have any idea what you do to me,' he laughed. It was a low rumbling sound that sent chills down her spine.

'I think I do,' she smiled shyly.

'And I think I should drive you to your brother's house right now,' he said, lifting his head away from her and reluctantly allowing their bodies to part.

'Should you be left alone tonight?' she questioned, refusing to totally relinquish her hold. 'Don't you think that since you're just out of hospital, someone should be here to keep a close watch over you?'

'How close?' Jet eyes held her captive as his hands moved possessively over her hips.

'Very close,' she breathed, as her body flamed beneath his touch. 'I don't think I mentioned if before, but I only have premonitions about people I love.'

Snuggled against Brad's body, Sara awoke the next morning to a peace she had never known. There was no doubt in her mind that she was exactly where she belonged.

'Good morning, sleepyhead,' he greeted her, kissing her hair while brushing some of the wayward strands from her face.

'Good morning,' she returned, turning her head into the warm flesh on which it rested to press her lips against his shoulder.

Catching her chin, he gently raised her face up to meet

his gaze. 'I hope you realise that you've compromised me completely,' he growled.

'I have?' she purred in mock innocence.

'Yes, you have, and there's only one way to compensate.'

'And what is that?' she asked, leaning up on an elbow and tracing the shape of his jaw with the tips of her fingers.

'You'll have to marry me immediately,' he demanded, catching her hand and carrying it to his mouth, where he nipped her fingers playfully.

'Speaking of immediately,' she said, suddenly stiffening, 'What time is it?'

'I've just proposed and the lady wants to know what time it is!' he mocked her, shaking his head sadly.

'I'm serious.' Sara tried to frown, but found herself placing a light kiss on his lips instead. Then, leaning over him to read the clock on the table, she gasped and started to climb out of bed, but he held her back.

'What's the rush? You haven't given me your answer. Will you marry me immediately?'

'Yes, any time you want—just let me get dressed. It's after nine and Steve could show up here at any minute,' she pleaded.

'No, he won't,' said Brad, trailing a line of kisses along her shoulder while continuing to hold her captive. 'I called him while you were still asleep.'

'You did what?' she demanded, catching the hint of mischief in his voice.

'I called and told him we were getting married and that I would not appreciate his barging in and interrupting us while we were discussing our wedding plans,' he elaborated, leaving her shoulder to tease a breast.

'What did he say?' she stammered.

'He said that once he knew about the premonitions, he

realised that this was inevitable. However, he was insistent that we should do more about a wedding than simply discuss it, so how does tomorrow suit you?'

'Tomorrow?' His moving sensually over her body was making thinking nearly impossible.

'Tomorrow for the wedding. Do you think Joanie could be ready by then?'

'That's not much time,' she murmured, attempting to concentrate.

Straightening away from her, he met her slightly dazed gaze. 'I want you with me always, Sara,' he growled, running his hand possessively along the length of her body. 'And I don't want to have to worry about an irate brother or mother breaking down my door. Then there's the matter of the little half-Yankees I want to have running around underfoot.'

'Tomorrow,' she agreed, trembling as his touch reawakened desire.

'Good,' he smiled. 'I was certain I could make you see it my way. Now it's time to take a little trip to the licence bureau.'

'Right this minute?' she questioned, running a hand over his chest.

'No, not right this minute,' he conceded huskily.